SIDDHARTHA

SIDDHARTHA
• AN INDIAN POEM •

HERMANN HESSE

Translated by Katja Pelzer

FALL RIVER PRESS

New York

FALL RIVER PRESS

New York

An Imprint of Sterling Publishing
1166 Avenue of the Americas
New York, NY 10036

The new translation used in this volume is based on
the original 1922 publication of the novel
by S. Fischer Verlag, Berlin.

ISBN 978-1-4351-5624-1

For information about custom editions, special sales, and premium and
corporate purchases, please contact Sterling Special Sales at 800-805-5489
or specialsales@sterlingpublishing.com.

Manufactured in the United States of America

2 4 6 8 10 9 7 5 3 1

www.sterlingpublishing.com

PART I

THE SON OF THE BRAHMIN

In the shade of the house, in the sunlight of the riverbank by the boats, in the shade of the sal wood, in the shade of the fig tree, Siddhartha, the handsome son of the Brahmin, the young falcon, grew up with his friend, Govinda, a Brahmin's son. Sunlight browned his fair shoulders on the riverbank, as he bathed, during the holy ablutions, during the holy sacrifices. Shade streamed into his black eyes in the mango grove, as the boys played, as his mother sang, during the holy sacrifices, during the teachings of his father, the scholar, and the conversations of the wise men. Siddhartha had long since been taking part in the wise men's conversations, practicing debate with Govinda, practicing with Govinda the art of contemplation, the duty of meditation. He had already learned to speak the Om silently, the word of words, to speak it silently into himself as he breathed in, to speak it silently out of himself as he breathed out, with his soul collected, his forehead surrounded by the luster of a clearly thinking mind. He had already learned to feel the presence of Atman in his innermost being, indestructible, at one with the universe.

7

Joy leaped into his father's heart when he saw the son, studious, thirsty for knowledge; he saw a great sage and priest growing within him, a prince among the Brahmins.

Delight leaped in his mother's breast when she saw him, when she saw him walking, sitting down, and standing up, Siddhartha, strong and handsome, walking on slender legs, greeting her with perfect grace.

Love stirred in the hearts of the young Brahmin daughters as Siddhartha walked through the alleys of the town, with his radiant brow, his regal eye, his narrow hips.

But more than anyone, he was loved by Govinda, his friend, the Brahmin's son. Govinda loved Siddhartha's eyes and lovely voice, he loved the way he walked and the perfect grace of his movements. He loved everything that Siddhartha did and said, and most of all he loved his mind, his noble, fiery thoughts, his fervent will, his high calling. Govinda knew: he would become no ordinary Brahmin, no idle sacrificial official, no greedy trader of incantations, no vain and vacant orator, neither a wicked and deceitful priest, nor a good and foolish sheep in the herd of many. No, and nor did he, Govinda, want to become an ordinary Brahmin, of which there were ten thousand. He wanted to follow Siddhartha, the beloved, the wonderful one. And if Siddhartha were someday to become a god, if he were someday to join the radiant ones, Govinda wanted to follow him, as his friend, as his companion, as his servant, as his spear-bearer, as his shadow.

Everyone loved Siddhartha. He brought everyone joy, gave everyone pleasure.

But he, Siddhartha, did not bring himself joy, he did not please himself. Walking on the rosy paths of the fig garden, sitting in the bluish shade of the grove of contemplation, washing his limbs in his daily bath of atonement, performing sacrifices in the deep shade of the mango wood, with gestures of perfect grace, loved by all, a joy to all, he bore no joy in his heart. Dreams came to him and restless thoughts came flowing from the water in the river, sparkling from the stars in the night, melted from the rays of the sun. Dreams came to him and unrest in his soul, smoked from the sacrifices, whispered from the verses of the Rig-Veda, trickled from the teachings of the old Brahmins.

Siddhartha had begun to nurture discontent within. He had begun to feel that his father's love, his mother's love, and also Govinda's love would not always and forever please him, pacify him, satiate him, suffice him. He had begun to sense that his venerable father and his other teachers, that all the wise Brahmins, had already conveyed to him the most and the best of their wisdom, that they had already poured their wealth into his waiting vessel and that the vessel was not full, his mind was not satisfied, his soul was not calm, his heart was not pacified. The ablutions were good but they were water, they did not wash away sin, they did not cure his mind's thirst, they did not dissolve his heart's fear. The sacrifices and the invocations of the gods were admirable—but was this all there was? Did the sacrifices bring happiness? And what about the gods? Was it really Prajapati who had created the world? Was it not Atman, He, the One and Only? Were the gods not shapes, created like me and you, subject to time, ephemeral? So was it good, was it right, was it a meaningful and noble act to sacrifice to the gods? Who else should receive sacrifices, who else deserve veneration other than He, the One, Atman? And where was Atman to be found, where did He reside, where did His eternal heart beat, where other than within one's own Self, within the innermost inde-structible core that everyone carries within? But where, where was this Self, this innermost core? It was not flesh and bone, it was not thought or consciousness, according to the wisest men's teachings. Where was it then, where? To reach this place, the Self, myself, Atman—was there another way worth seeking? Oh, and no one showed the way, no one knew it, not his father, not the teachers and wise men, not the holy sacrificial verses! They knew everything, the Brahmins and their holy books, they knew everything, they had concerned themselves with everything and more than everything, the creation of the world, the origin of speech, of food, of inhaling, of exhaling, of the orders of the senses, of the deeds of the gods—they knew an infinite amount. But was all this knowledge valuable if one did not know the One and Only, the most important, the only important thing?

Of course many of the holy books' verses, above all the Upanishads of Sama-Veda, spoke of this innermost and ulti-mate thing—magnificent verses. "Your soul is the entire world" was written there; and it was written that in sleep, in deep sleep, one enters one's innermost core and dwells in Atman. Wonderful wisdom was in these verses, all the knowledge of the wisest men was collected here in magical words, as pure as honey gathered by bees. No, the immense amount of insight gathered and preserved here by countless generations of wise Brahmins was not to be disregarded. But where were the Brahmins, where the priests, where the wise men or penitents who had succeeded not only in acquiring this deepest knowledge but also in living it? Where was the master who was able to magically shift his ability to dwell in Atman during sleep to the waking state, to life, to all comings and goings, to every word and deed? Siddhartha knew many venerable Brahmins, above all his father, a pure, scholarly, highly venerable man. Worthy of admiration was his father, calm and regal was his demeanor, pure was his life, wise were his words, fine and noble thoughts resided in his brow. But even he, who knew so much, did he live in bliss, did he live in peace? Was he not also a mere seeker, plagued by thirst? Was he, a thirsty man, not compelled to drink again and again from the holy springs, from the sacrifices, from the books, from the dialogues of the Brahmins? Why was he, who was without fault, compelled to wash himself of sin day after day, strive for purification day after day, every day anew? Was Atman not within him, did the spring's source not flow in his own heart? This is what must be found, the source in oneself, this must be made one's own! Everything else was seeking, detour, deviation.

These were Siddhartha's thoughts, this was his thirst, this his suffering.

He often spoke the words from a Chandogya Upanishad to himself: "In truth, the Brahmin's name is Satyam—truly, he who knows this enters the heavenly world every day." It often seemed to be near, the heavenly world, but he had never quite reached it, never quenched the final thirst. And of all the wise and wisest men he knew and whose teachings he enjoyed, none among them had quite reached it, the heavenly world; none had completely quenched it, the eternal thirst.

"Govinda," said Siddhartha to his friend, "Govinda, dear friend, come with me under the banyan tree. Let us practice meditation."

They walked to the banyan tree, they sat down, here Siddhartha, Govinda twenty steps further. As he sat down, ready to speak the Om, Siddhartha repeated the verse, murmuring:

> Om is the bow, the soul is the arrow,
> Brahman is the arrow's mark,
> This should be struck persistently.

When the usual time for meditation had passed, Govinda rose. Evening had arrived. It was time to perform the evening ablutions. He called Siddhartha's name. Siddhartha did not answer. Siddhartha sat immersed, his eyes rigidly focused on a very distant point, the tip of his tongue protruding slightly from between his teeth; he did not seem to be breathing. So he sat, shrouded in meditation, thinking Om, his soul an arrow sent forth to Brahman.

Once, Samanas had passed through Siddhartha's town: ascetics on a pilgrimage, three gaunt and extinguished men, neither old nor young, with dusty and bloody shoulders, nearly naked and singed by the sun, surrounded by solitude, alien and hostile to the world, strangers—haggard jackals in the realm of men. Behind them blew hotly the scent of quiet passion, of devastating service, of ruthless elimination of Self.

In the evening, after the hour of contemplation, Siddhartha said to Govinda: "Tomorrow morning, my friend, Siddhartha will go to the Samanas. He will become a Samana."

Govinda turned pale as he heard the words and read in his friend's motionless face the resolution, as indivertible as the arrow shot from the bow. Govinda recognized at once and at first glance: now it is beginning, now Siddhartha is going his way, now his destiny has begun to sprout, and with his, mine as well. And he became as pale as a dry banana peel.

"O Siddhartha," he cried, "will you father allow it?"

Siddhartha looked at him as one who is awakening. Like an arrow he read in Govinda's soul the fear, read the resignation.

"O Govinda," he said softly, "let us not waste words. Tomorrow, at daybreak, I will begin the life of the Samanas. Speak no more of it."

Siddhartha entered the room where his father was sitting on a mat made of bast. He stepped behind his father and stood still until his father felt that someone was standing behind him. The Brahmin spoke: "Is it you, Siddhartha? Then say what you have come to say."

Said Siddhartha: "With your permission, my father. I have come to tell you that I wish to leave your house tomorrow and join the ascetics. To become a Samana is my desire. May my father not be opposed."

The Brahmin was silent, and remained silent for so long that the stars traveled across the small window and changed their shape before the silence in the room came to an end. Mute and motionless stood the son with crossed arms, mute and motionless sat the father on the mat, and the stars traveled across the sky. Then the father spoke: "It does not suit the Brahmin to speak sharp and angry words. But there is displeasure in my heart. I do not wish to hear this request from your lips a second time."

The Brahmin rose slowly; Siddhartha stood silently with crossed arms.

"What are you waiting for?" asked the father.

Said Siddhartha: "You know."

With displeasure, the father left the room; with displeasure, he sought his bed and lay down.

After an hour, as sleep would not close his eyes, the Brahmin rose, walked back and forth, walked out of the house. He looked through the small window into the room, saw Siddhartha standing there, with crossed arms, unmoved. His fair robe shimmered pale. With disquiet in his heart, the father returned to his bed.

After an hour, as sleep would not come to him, the Brahmin rose again, walked back and forth, walked in front of the house, saw that the moon had risen. He looked through the small window into the room, saw Siddhartha standing there, with crossed arms, unmoved, his bare shins reflecting the moonlight. With concern in his heart, the father returned to his bed.

And he came again after one hour, and came again after two hours, looked through the small window, saw Siddhartha standing, in the light of the moon, the light of the stars, in the darkness. And he returned from hour to hour, in silence, looked into the room, saw his son standing unmoved; his heart filled with anger, his heart filled with disquiet, his heart filled with hesitation, his heart filled with sorrow.

And in the night's final hour, before the day began, he returned again, entered the room, saw the youth standing, who seemed tall and unfamiliar to him.

"Siddhartha," he said, "what are you waiting for?"

"You know."

"Will you continue to stand and wait, until day comes, afternoon comes, evening comes?"

"I will stand and wait."

"You will grow tired, Siddhartha."

"I will grow tired."

"You will fall asleep, Siddhartha."

"I will not fall asleep."

"You will die, Siddhartha."

"I will die."

"And you would rather die than obey your father?"

"Siddhartha has always obeyed his father."

"So you will give up your plan?"

"Siddhartha will do as his father says."

The first light of day fell into the room. The Brahmin saw that Siddhartha's knees trembled slightly. In Siddhartha's face he saw no trembling, the eyes looked into the distance. The father then realized that Siddhartha had already ceased to reside with him in the place of his birth, that he had already left him.

The father touched Siddhartha's shoulder.

"You shall go to the forest and become a Samana," he said. "If you find bliss in the forest, come and teach me bliss. If you find disappointment, return and let us sacrifice to the gods together again. Now go and kiss your mother, tell her where you are going. For me it is time to go to the river and perform the first ablution."

He removed his hand from his son's shoulder and walked out. Siddhartha stumbled sideways as he tried to walk. He subdued his limbs, bowed to his father, and went to his mother to do as his father had said.

At first daylight, he slowly left the still-silent city on stiff legs; a shadow that had been cowering by the last hut rose to join the pilgrim—Govinda.

"You have come," Siddhartha said and smiled.

"I have come," said Govinda.

AMONG THE SAMANAS

In the evening of that day, they caught up to the ascetics, the gaunt Samanas, and offered them companionship and obedience. They were accepted.

Siddhartha gave his robe to a poor Brahmin on the road. He now wore only a loincloth and an unsewn, earth-colored cloak. He ate only once a day and never food that had been cooked. He fasted for fifteen days. He fasted for twenty-eight days. The flesh vanished from his thighs and cheeks. Hot dreams flickered from his enlarged eyes; on his withered fingers grew long nails, and on his chin, a dry, coarse beard. His gaze became icy when he encountered women; his mouth twitched in contempt when he passed through a town with elegantly dressed people. He saw traders trading, princes going to hunt, mourners weeping for their dead, whores offering themselves, doctors tending to the sick, priests setting the day for sowing, lovers making love, mothers nursing their children—and all this was not worthy of his gaze, it all lied, it all stank, it all stank of lies, it all feigned meaning and joy and beauty, and it was all unacknowledged decay. The world tasted bitter. Life was agony.

Siddhartha saw a goal before him, only one: to become empty, empty of thirst, empty of desire, empty of dream, empty of joy and sorrow. To die away from himself, to no longer be Self, to find peace with an emptied heart, to be open to wonder in thought freed of Self, this was his goal. When the Self had been overcome and perished, when every desire and urge in his heart had fallen silent, then the ultimate had to awake, the innermost of his being, that which is no longer Self—the great secret.

Siddhartha stood silently beneath the burning sun, glowing with pain, glowing with thirst, and stood until he felt pain and thirst no longer. He stood silently during the rains, the water dripping from his hair over freezing shoulders, over freezing hips and legs, and the penitent stood until shoulders and legs no longer froze, until they fell silent, until they were still. He crouched silently in the thornbushes, blood seeped from his burning skin, pus from his boils, and Siddhartha remained rigid, remained motionless, until no more blood flowed, until nothing pricked, until nothing burned.

Siddhartha sat upright and learned to breathe sparingly, learned to do with little breath, learned to suppress his breathing. Beginning with his breath, he learned to calm his heartbeat, learned to decrease the beats of his heart, until they were few and almost none.

Taught by the eldest of the Samanas, Siddhartha practiced elimination of Self, practiced meditation, according to the Samana rules. A heron flew over the bamboo forest—and Siddhartha let the heron into his soul, flew over forest and mountains, was the heron, ate fish, suffered heron hunger, spoke heron squawks, died a heron death. A dead jackal lay on the sandy bank, and Siddhartha's soul slipped inside the carcass, was the dead jackal, lay on the shore, became bloated, stank, decayed, became dismembered by hyenas, was skinned by the vultures, became skeleton, became dust, blew into the fields. And Siddhartha's soul returned, had died, had decayed, had dispersed, had tasted the blurred frenzy of the cycle, waited with new thirst like a hunter for the gap where one could escape the cycle, where the end of the causes, an eternity free of suffering, would begin. He killed his senses, he killed his memory, he slipped from his Self into a thousand foreign shapes, was animal, was carrion, was stone, was wood, was water, and each time found himself waking again, the sun shining or the moon, was himself again, swung in the cycle, felt thirst, overcame the thirst, felt new thirst.

Siddhartha learned many things among the Samanas, he learned to walk many paths that led away from the Self. He walked the path to elimination of Self through pain, through the voluntary suffering and overcoming of pain, of hunger, of thirst, of fatigue. He walked the path to elimination of Self through meditation, by emptying his mind of all perceptions through thought. He learned to walk these and other paths, left his Self a thousand times, remained for hours and days on end in his non-Self. But just as these paths led away from the Self, their final destination always led back to the Self. Even if Siddhartha escaped the Self a thousand times, lingering in nothingness, in animals, in stone, inevitable was the return, inescapable the hour in which he found himself again, in sunlight or in moonlight, in shade or in rain, and was Self and Siddhartha again, and felt again the agony of the imposed cycle.

Govinda, his shadow, lived beside him, walked the same paths, subjected himself to the same exertions. They rarely spoke to each other about anything other than that required by their duty and exercises. Occasionally the two of them walked through the villages to beg for food for themselves and their teachers.

"What do you think, Govinda," Siddhartha said once while begging, "what do you think? Have we made progress? Have we reached goals?"

Govinda answered: "We have learned, and we continue to learn. You shall become a great Samana, Siddhartha. You have mastered every exercise quickly, the old Samanas have often admired you. One day you will be a holy man, O Siddhartha."

Said Siddhartha: "It does not appear so to me, my friend. That which I have learned until today among the Samanas, O Govinda, I could have learned more quickly and easily. I could have learned it in any bar in the whores' district, my friend, among the cart drivers and gamblers."

Said Govinda: "Siddhartha is joking with me. How could you have learned to meditate, to hold your breath, to be callous to hunger and pain among such miserable creatures?"

And Siddhartha said quietly, as though speaking to himself: "What is meditation? What is leaving the body? What is fasting? What is holding one's breath? It is escape from the Self, it is a brief flight from the agony of being one's Self, it is a brief numbing of the pain and senselessness of life. This same escape, this same brief numbing, is found by the ox driver at the inn when he drinks a few bowls of rice wine or fermented coconut milk. Then he no longer feels his Self, then he no longer feels the pains of life, then he finds brief numbness. Dozed off over his bowl of rice wine, he finds the same thing that Siddhartha and Govinda find when they escape their bodies in long exercises and linger in the non-Self. This is how it is, O Govinda."

Said Govinda: "So you say, O friend, and yet you know that Siddhartha is no ox driver and a Samana no drunkard. Surely the drinker finds numbness, surely he finds a brief escape and rest, but he returns from the delusion to find everything as it was before, has not grown wiser, has not gathered insight, has not ascended to a higher rung."

And Siddhartha said with a smile: "I do not know, I have never been a drinker. But that I, Siddhartha, only find brief numbness in my exercises and meditations and am as far from wisdom, from redemption, as I was as a child in the womb, this I know, O Govinda, this I know."

And on another occasion, as Siddhartha left the forest with Govinda to beg for some food for their brothers and teachers in the village, Siddhartha began to speak and said: "And now, O Govinda, are we still on the right path? Are we still approaching insight? Are we approaching redemption? Or are we perhaps going in circles—we, who intended to escape the cycle?"

Said Govinda: "We have learned much, Siddhartha, and much remains to be learned. We are not going in circles, we are rising; the circle is a spiral, we have already ascended many rungs."

Siddhartha answered: "How old do you think our oldest Samana is, our venerable teacher?"

Said Govinda: "Our eldest may be sixty years old."

And Siddhartha: "He is sixty years old and has not reached Nirvana. He will become seventy and eighty, and you and I, we will also become old and we will practice, and fast, and meditate. But Nirvana will not be reached, not by him, not by us. O Govinda, I believe that of all the Samanas alive, maybe not one, not one will reach Nirvana. We find consolations, we find numbness, we learn skills with which to deceive ourselves. But the essence, the Path of Paths, we do not find."

"May you not speak such terrifying words, Siddhartha!" said Govinda. "How can it be that among so many learned men, among so many Brahmins, among so many strict and venerable Samanas, among so many seekers, so many sincerely devoted, so many holy men, none can find the Path of Paths?"

But Siddhartha said, in a voice that held as much sadness as mockery, with a soft, a somewhat sad, a somewhat mocking voice: "Soon, Govinda, your friend will leave this path of the Samanas that he has traveled with you for so long. I suffer thirst, O Govinda, and on this long Samana path my thirst has not become any smaller. I have always thirsted for insight, I have always been full of questions. I questioned the Brahmins, year after year, and questioned the Vedas, year after year. Perhaps, O Govinda, it would have been just as good, it would have been just as clever and just as beneficial to have questioned the hornbill or the chimpanzees. It has taken me a long time to learn—and I am not yet finished learning, O Govinda—that one can learn nothing! This thing, I believe, that we call 'learning' does not in fact exist. There is, O my friend, only one knowledge: it is everywhere, it is Atman, it is in me and in you and in every being. And so I am beginning to believe that this knowledge has no worse enemy than the desire for knowledge, than learning."

At this, Govinda stopped on the path, raised his hands, and said: "Please, Siddhartha, may you not frighten your friend with such speech! Truly, your words awaken fear in my heart. And just consider: what would become of the holiness of prayer, what would become of the venerability of the Brahmin class, of the holiness of the Samanas, if it were as you say, if there were no learning?! What, O Siddhartha, what would become of all this, all that is holy on earth, that is valuable, that is venerable?!

And Govinda murmured a verse to himself, a verse from an Upanishad:

> He of meditative, clarified mind,
> who immerses himself in Atman,
> Inexpressible through words is his heart's bliss.

But Siddhartha was silent. He thought of the words Govinda had said to him, and thought the words through to their end.

Yes, he thought, standing with his head bowed, what would remain of all that seemed holy to us? What remains? What proves itself to be true? And he shook his head.

After the two youths had been among the Samanas and shared their exercises for about three years, news reached them through several roundabout routes—a rumor, a legend that one had arrived, named Gautama, the Sublime One, the Buddha, who had overcome within himself the suffering of the world and brought the wheel of rebirths to a standstill. He was traveling through the country, teaching, surrounded by disciples, without possessions, without a home, without a wife, in the yellow cloak of an ascetic but with a cheerful brow, a Blessed One, and Brahmins and princes bowed before him and became his pupils.

This legend, this rumor, this myth resounded, drifted fragrantly through the air, here and there; in the cities the Brahmins spoke of it, in the forest the Samanas spoke of it, again and again the name Gautama, the Buddha, reached the youths' ears, in good will and bad, in praise and condemnation.

As if in a land ravaged by the plague, in which news emerges that here and there is a man, a wise man, a master, whose word and breath would suffice to heal all those afflicted with pestilence; and as if this news were then to traverse the country and everyone were to speak of it, many to believe, many to doubt, and many to set forth at once to find the wise man, the helper— in such a way was the country traversed by this legend, this fragrant legend of Gautama, the Buddha, the wise man from the Sakya clan. He possessed ultimate insight, said the believers, he remembered his previous lives, he had reached Nirvana and never again returned to the cycle, would never again be submerged in the turbid stream of shapes. Many wonderful and incredible things were told of him: he had performed miracles, had conquered the devil, had spoken with the gods. But his enemies and disbelievers said that this Gautama was a vain seducer, that he whiled away his days in luxury, scorned the sacrifices, was unlearned, and knew neither exercise nor self-castigation.

Sweet was the sound of these legends of Buddha, magic was the fragrance of these reports. The world was ailing, after all, life was difficult to bear—and behold, here a fountain seemed to spring, here a messenger's call seemed to sound, consoling, mild, full of noble promises. Everywhere the rumor of Buddha resounded, everywhere in the lands of India the youths listened keenly, felt longing, felt hope, and among the Brahmin sons in the cities and villages every pilgrim and stranger was welcome who brought news of him, the Sublime One, the Sakyamuni.

The legend had also made its way to the Samanas in the forest, also to Siddhartha, also to Govinda, gradually, in drops, each drop heavy with hope, each drop heavy with doubt. They spoke little of it, as the eldest of the Samanas was no friend of this legend. He had heard that this alleged Buddha had once been an ascetic, had lived in the forest, but had turned back to a life of luxury and worldly pleasures, and he thought little of this Gautama.

"O Siddhartha," Govinda once said to his friend, "today I was in the village and a Brahmin invited me to enter his house, and in his house was a Brahmin's son from Magadha who had seen the Buddha with his own eyes and had heard him teach. Truly, my chest ached with every breath, and I thought to myself: May I, may we both, Siddhartha and I, also live to hear the Teaching from the lips of that Perfect One! Speak, friend, should we not also go there and hear the Teaching from the lips of Buddha?"

Said Siddhartha: "I always thought, O Govinda, that Govinda would stay with the Samanas, I always believed it was his goal to become sixty and seventy years old and to continue to practice the skills and exercises that adorn the Samana. But it appears that I know Govinda too little, I know little of his heart. So now, dearest friend, you wish to take a new path and go to the place where the Buddha is proclaiming his teaching."

Said Govinda: "You choose to mock me. Mock me if you like, Siddhartha! But has a longing, a desire to hear this Teaching not also awoken within you? And did you not once say to me that you will not be traveling the path of the Samanas much longer?"

Siddhartha then laughed, in his way, whereby the tone of his voice took on a trace of sadness and a trace of mockery, and said: "You have spoken well, Govinda, and remembered correctly. But may you also remember the other words that you heard from me, that I have become wary and tired of teachings and learning and that I have little faith in words that come to us from teachers. But very well, dear friend, I am willing to hear this Teaching—although I believe in my heart that we have already tasted this Teaching's best fruit."

Said Govinda: "Your willingness delights my heart. But tell me, how can that be possible? How could the Teaching of Gautama have already revealed its best fruit to us before we have heard it?"

Said Siddhartha: "Let us savor this fruit and wait to see what comes next, O Govinda! But this fruit, which we can already thank Gautama for today, is that he is calling us away from the Samanas! Whether he has other and better things to give us, O friend, let us wait with calm hearts and see."

On this same day, Siddhartha informed the eldest of the Samanas of his decision to leave him. He informed him, the eldest, with the courtesy and modesty that is befitting of young men and pupils. The Samana, however, became enraged that the two youths wanted to leave him, and spoke loudly, and used coarse, scolding words.

Govinda was startled and at a loss, but Siddhartha leaned his mouth to Govinda's ear and whispered to him: "Now I will show the old man that I have learned something from him."

By positioning himself directly in front of the Samana, his soul collected, he captured the old man's gaze with his own, transfixed him, made him silent, conquered his will, subjected him to his own will, ordered him to silently do as he was asked. The old man became silent, his eyes became rigid, his will paralyzed, his arms dangled down, he had powerlessly succumbed to Siddhartha's enchantment. Siddhartha's thoughts now took possession of the Samana's; he had to do as they commanded. So the old man bowed many times, made blessing gestures, stuttered a pious wish for a good journey. And the youths returned the bows in gratitude, returned the good wishes, said farewell, and departed.

On the road, Govinda said: "O Siddhartha, you learned more among the Samanas than I knew. It is difficult, it is very difficult to enchant an old Samana. Had you remained there, you would surely have soon learned to walk upon water."

"I do not wish to walk upon water," said Siddhartha. "Let old Samanas content themselves with such tricks!"

GAUTAMA

In the city of Savathi every child knew the name of the Sublime Buddha and every house was equipped to fill the alms bowl of Gautama's disciples, the silent beseechers. Near the city lay Gautama's favorite residence, the Jetavana Grove, which the wealthy merchant Anathapindika, a devoted admirer of the Sublime One, had bestowed upon him and his followers.

This was the place that had been referred to in all tales and replies given to the two young ascetics in their search for Gautama's whereabouts. And when they arrived in Savathi, they were already offered food at the first house whose door they stopped in front of to beg, and they accepted the food, and Siddhartha asked the woman who handed him the food:

"Charitable lady, we would like to know where the Buddha resides, the Most Venerable One, for we are two Samanas from the forest and have come to see him, the Perfect One, and to hear the Teaching from his lips."

Said the woman: "Indeed you have landed here in the right place, Samanas from the forest. In Jetavana, in the garden of Anathapindika, is where the Sublime One resides. There, pilgrims, you may spend the night, as there is enough room for the countless numbers who converge on this place to hear the Teaching from his lips."

At this, Govinda rejoiced, and full of joy, he cried: "Wonderful, then our goal has been reached and our journey is at an end! But tell us, mother of the pilgrims, do you know him, the Buddha, have you seen him with your own eyes?"

Said the woman: "I have seen him many times, the Sublime One. On many a day I have seen him walking through the streets, silently, in a yellow cloak, silently holding out his alms bowl at the house doors, carrying the full bowl away."

Govinda listened with delight and wanted to ask and hear much more. But Siddhartha said they must continue on. They gave thanks and left and hardly needed to ask the way, as more than a few pilgrims and also monks from Gautama's fellowship were on their way to Jetavana. And as they arrived there at night, there were continuous arrivals and the calls and conversations of those seeking and finding lodging. The two Samanas, accustomed to life in the forest, found shelter quickly and silently and rested there until morning.

As the sun rose, they were amazed to see what a large crowd of believers and spectators had spent the night there. Monks in yellow robes strolled through all the paths of the magnificent grove; they sat here and there beneath the trees, absorbed in contemplation, or in spiritual conversation. The shaded gardens appeared to be a city, full of people, swarming like bees. Most of the monks set forth with their alms bowls to collect food in the city for the midday meal, the only one of the day.

Even the Buddha himself, the Enlightened One, had the custom of begging for alms every morning.

Siddhartha saw him and recognized him at once, as though he had been pointed to by a god. He saw him, a simple man in a yellow cowl, carrying the alms bowl in his hand as he walked silently along.

"Look!" Siddhartha said quietly to Govinda. "This one here is the Buddha."

Govinda looked attentively at the monk in the yellow cowl who did not seem discernible in any way from the hundreds of other monks. And soon Govinda saw as well: this is the one. And they followed after him and observed him.

The Buddha went his way modestly and absorbed in thought. His calm face was neither cheerful nor sad; it seemed to be softly smiling inwards. With a concealed smile, quiet, calm, not unlike a healthy child, the Buddha walked, wore his robe, and set his feet just as all his monks, according to precise rules. But his face and his step, his quietly lowered gaze, his quietly dangling hand, and even every finger on his quietly dangling hand, spoke peace, spoke perfection, did not seek, did not imitate, breathed gently in an unwithering serenity, in an unwithering light, an unassailable peace.

And so walked Gautama, toward the city, to gather alms. And the two Samanas recognized him solely by the perfection of his serenity, by the tranquility of his figure, in which no seeking, no want, no imitation, no striving was to be found, only light and peace.

"Today we will hear the Teaching from his lips," said Govinda.

Siddhartha gave no reply. He was not very curious about the Teaching, he did not believe that they would teach him anything new; after all, he, like Govinda, had heard the contents of the Buddha's Teaching again and again, albeit from second- and third-hand accounts. But he looked attentively at Gautama's head, at his shoulders, at his feet, at his quietly dangling hand, and it seemed to him that every part of every finger on this hand was teaching; they spoke, breathed, radiated, glistened truth. This man, this Buddha, was veritable down to the gestures of his smallest finger. This man was holy. Never before had Siddhartha admired a man like this, never before had he loved a man as he did this one.

The two followed the Buddha to the city and turned back silently, as they themselves intended to refrain from food that day. They watched Gautama return, watched him take his meal among his disciples—what he ate would not have satiated a bird—and watched him retire to the shade of the mango trees.

But in the evening, as the heat subsided and everyone in the camp became lively and gathered together, they heard the Buddha teach. They heard his voice, and it too was perfect, perfectly calm, full of peace. Gautama taught the doctrine of suffering, of the origin of suffering, of the path to the elimination of suffering. Calmly flowing and clear were his quiet words. Suffering was life, full of suffering was the world, but deliverance from suffering had been found: deliverance would be found by he who walks the path of the Buddha.

In a gentle but firm voice the Sublime One spoke, taught the four main principles, taught the eightfold path; patiently, he went the familiar path of the Teaching, the examples, the repetitions, his voice levitated bright and still above the listeners, like a light, like a starry sky.

As the Buddha ended his speech—night had already come—many a pilgrim stepped forward and asked for acceptance into the fellowship, took refuge in the Teaching. And Gautama took them in by saying: "You have listened to the Teaching, it has been proclaimed. Join us then and walk in holiness, put an end to all suffering."

And, lo! Govinda also stepped forward, the shy one, and said: "I, too, take refuge in the Sublime One and his Teaching," and asked for acceptance into the fellowship, and was accepted.

Afterwards, as the Buddha had retired for the night, Govinda turned to Siddhartha and spoke eagerly: "Siddhartha, it is not fitting for me to reproach you. Both of us have heard the Sublime One, both of us have heard his Teaching. Govinda has heard the Teaching, he has taken refuge in it. But you, honored friend, do you not also want to travel the path of redemption? Do you want to hesitate, do you want to keep waiting?

Siddhartha awoke as though from sleep as he took in Govinda's words. He gazed at Govinda's face for a long time. Then he spoke softly, with a voice free of mockery: "Govinda, my friend, now you have taken the step, now you have chosen the path. You have always been my friend, O Govinda, you have always walked one step behind me. I often thought: Will Govinda not one day take a step alone, without me, from within his own soul? And see now, you have become a man and are choosing your own path. May you travel it to the end, O my friend! May you find redemption!"

Govinda, who did not yet fully understand, repeated his question with a touch of impatience: "Please speak, I beg you, dear friend! Tell me, as it can not be otherwise, that you, my learned friend, will take your refuge in the sublime Buddha!"

Siddhartha laid his hand on Govinda's shoulder: "You did not hear my blessing, O Govinda. I will repeat it: May you travel this path to the end! May you find redemption!"

At this moment, Govinda realized that his friend had left him, and he began to weep.

"Siddhartha!" he cried mournfully.

Siddhartha spoke kindly to him: "Do not forget, Govinda, that you now belong to the Buddha's Samanas! You have renounced birthplace and parents, renounced heritage and property, renounced your own will, renounced friendship. This is the will of the Teaching, this is the will of the Sublime One. This is what you yourself have chosen. Tomorrow, O Govinda, I will leave you."

For a long time the friends strolled through the grove, for a long time they lay and did not find sleep. And over and over Govinda urged his friend to tell him why he did not want to take his refuge in Gautama's Teaching, which flaw he found in this Teaching. But Siddhartha dismissed him each time and said: "Be content, Govinda! The Teaching of the Sublime One is very good, how should I find a flaw in it?"

In the earliest morning, a follower of Buddha, one of his eldest monks, walked through the garden and called all the novices who had taken refuge in the Teaching to him in order to give them their yellow robes, and he instructed them in the first Teachings and duties of their order. Govinda tore himself away, embraced the friend of his youth one last time, and joined the procession of novices.

But Siddhartha walked through the grove, deep in thought.

There he encountered Gautama, the Sublime One, and as he greeted him with reverence and saw the Buddha's gaze so full of kindness and tranquility, the youth found his courage and asked the Venerable One for permission to speak to him. The Sublime One silently nodded his consent.

Said Siddhartha: "Yesterday, O Sublime One, I was granted the privilege of hearing your wondrous Teaching. Together with my friend, I came from far away to hear this Teaching. And now my friend will remain among your followers, he has taken his refuge in you. I, however, will begin my pilgrimage anew."

"As you please," said the Sublime One politely.

"My words are far too bold," Siddhartha continued, "but I do not wish to leave the Sublime One before I have sincerely shared my thoughts with him. Will the Venerable One lend me his ear for one more moment?"

The Buddha silently nodded his consent.

Said Siddhartha: "There is one thing about your Teaching, Most Venerable One, that I admired above all. Everything in your Teaching is completely clear, is proven; you portray the world as a perfect chain, never and nowhere interrupted, as an eternal chain, forged by linking causes and effects. Never before has this been so clearly seen, never has it been so irrefutably

presented; every Brahmin's heart must surely beat faster when
he, through your Teaching, beholds the world as perfect coherence, uninterrupted, clear as a crystal, not dependent upon
chance, not dependent upon gods. Whether this world is good
or evil, whether life in it is sorrow or joy, may remain unde-
cided; it may be that this is not essential—but the unity of
the world, the coherence of all events, all things big and small
being encompassed by the same current, in the same law of
causes, of becoming and of dying, this shines brightly from
your sublime Teaching, O Perfect One. But now, according to
your same Teaching, this unity and consistency of all things
is nevertheless interrupted at one point. Through a small gap
something foreign flows into this world of unity, something
new, something that was not there before and that cannot be
shown and cannot be proven: this is your Teaching about overcoming the world, about deliverance. With this small gap, with
this small breach, the entire eternal and uniform law of the
world is shattered and rendered invalid. May you forgive me
for voicing this objection."

Silently, Gautama had listened to him, unmoved. In his
kind, in his polite and clear voice, the Perfect One now spoke:
"You have heard the Teaching, O Brahmin's son, and you have
done well to contemplate it so deeply. You have found a gap
in it, a flaw. May you continue to contemplate it. But beware,
inquisitive one, of the thicket of opinions and disputes over
words. Opinions are of no account, they may be pretty or ugly,
clever or foolish, anyone can adhere to or reject them. The
Teaching that you heard from me, however, is not my opinion,

its aim is not to explain the world to the inquisitive. It has a different aim; its aim is deliverance from suffering. This is what Gautama teaches, nothing else."

"May you not be angry with me, O Sublime One," said the youth. "It was not to seek dispute with you, over words that I spoke to you in this way. Indeed, you are right, opinions are of no account. But let me say this one last thing: not for a moment have I doubted you. I have not doubted for a moment that you are Buddha, that you have reached the goal, the highest goal, that so many thousands of Brahmins and Brahmins' sons are searching for. You have found deliverance from death. It came to you from your own seeking, on your own path, through thought, through meditation, through insight, through enlightenment. It did not come to you through teachings! And—such is my thought, O Sublime One—no one will attain deliverance through teachings! To no one, O Venerable One, will you be able to convey in words and through teaching what happened to you in the hour of your enlightenment! Much is contained in the Teaching of the enlightened Buddha, many they teach to live righteously, to shun evil. But one thing is not contained in this Teaching that is so clear, so venerable: it does not contain the secret of what the Sublime One himself has experienced, he alone among the hundreds of thousands. This is what I thought and realized when I heard the Teaching. This is why I am continuing my journey—not to seek a different, a better teaching, as I know there is none, but to leave all teachings and all teachers and to reach my goal alone or to die. But I will think of this day often, O Sublime One, and this hour when my eyes beheld a holy man."

The eyes of the Buddha gazed calmly at the ground; his impenetrable face shone calmly in perfect tranquility.

"May your thoughts," said the Venerable One slowly, "not be mistakes! May you reach your goal! But tell me: have you seen the large crowd of my Samanas, my many brothers who have taken refuge in the Teaching? And do you believe, unknown Samana, do you believe that they would all be better off if they were to leave the Teaching and return to the life of the world and desires?"

"Far be it for me to think such a thought," cried Siddhartha. "May they all remain faithful to the Teaching, may they all reach their goals! It is not my place to judge the life of another. Solely for myself, for myself alone, must I judge, must I choose, must I reject. Deliverance from the Self is what we Samanas are seeking, O Sublime One. If I were one of your disciples, O Venerable One, I fear it could happen that my Self would only seemingly, only deceptively, find peace and be delivered, while in truth it would live on and grow, as I would have turned the Teaching, my discipleship, my love for you, the fellowship of monks into my Self!"

With a half smile, with an unshaken brightness and friendliness, Gautama looked the stranger in the eye and took leave of him with a barely visible gesture.

"You are clever, O Samana," said the Venerable One. "You know how to speak cleverly, my friend. Beware of too much cleverness!"

The Buddha wandered off, and his gaze and half smile remained forever engraved in Siddhartha's memory.

Never have I seen a man gaze and smile, sit and walk in such a way, he thought. I would truly like to be able to gaze and smile, sit and walk like that, so freely, so venerably, so covertly, so openly, so childishly and mysteriously. Truly, only the man who has reached the innermost core of his being gazes and walks that way. Yes, I too will seek to reach the innermost core of my being. I have seen one man, Siddhartha thought, one single man for whom I had to cast down my eyes. I will no longer cast down my eyes for anyone, for no one else. No other teaching will allure me, as this man's Teaching has not allured me.

The Buddha has robbed me, thought Siddhartha, he has robbed me and yet given me even more. He has robbed me of my friend, he who believed in me and who now believes in him, he who was my shadow and who is now Gautama's shadow. But he has given me Siddhartha, he has given me myself.

AWAKENING

As Siddhartha left the grove in which the Buddha, the Perfect One, remained, in which Govinda remained, he felt that his previous life had also remained behind him in this grove, parted from him. He contemplated this sensation, which filled him entirely, as he slowly walked on. He contemplated deeply, he let himself sink as through deep waters until he reached the ground of this sensation, the place where the causes lay; for recognizing causes, it seemed to him, is the essence of thinking, and only in this way can sensations become insight and not be lost, but become entities and begin to radiate that which is within them.

Siddhartha thought while slowly walking on. He realized that he was no longer a youth but had become a man. He realized that one thing had left him, as a snake is left by its old skin, that one thing was no longer within him that had accompanied him throughout his entire youth and been a part of him: the desire to have teachers and listen to their teachings. He had left the last teacher who appeared on his path; even him, the greatest and wisest teacher, the holiest, Buddha, he had had to separate from, had not been able to accept his Teaching.

Walking on more slowly, the thinker asked himself: "But what is it that you sought to learn from teachings and from teachers, and what were those who have taught you so much not able to teach you after all?" And he found: "It was the Self whose meaning and nature I sought to learn. It was the Self that I sought to get away from, that I sought to overcome. But I was unable to overcome it. I could only deceive it, flee from it, hide from it. Truly, nothing in the world has occupied my thoughts as much as my own Self, this mystery that I live, that I am one and separated and isolated from everyone else, that I am Siddhartha! There is nothing in the world that I know less about than myself, about Siddhartha!"

Walking on slowly, the thinker now stopped, gripped by this thought, and at once a different thought sprang forth, a new thought which was: "That I know nothing of myself. That Siddhartha has remained so foreign and unknown to me, is due to one reason, one reason alone: I was afraid of myself, I was fleeing from myself! I sought Atman, I sought Brahman, I was willing to dismember and peel apart my Self in order to find the core of all layers in its unknown heart, Atman, life, the divine, the ultimate. But in doing so, I lost myself."

Siddhartha opened his eyes and looked around. A smile filled his face and a deep sensation of awakening from a long dream flooded through him to his toes. And at once he began to walk again, to walk swiftly, like a man who knows what he must do.

"Oh," he thought, breathing deeply again, "I will not let Siddhartha slip away from me again! No longer will I begin my thinking and my life with Atman and the world's suffering. I will no longer kill and dismember myself in order to discover a secret behind the ruins. Neither Yoga-Veda shall teach me, nor Atharva-Veda, nor the ascetics, nor any other teaching. I want to learn from myself, be my own follower, get to know myself, the secret Siddhartha."

He looked around as though he were seeing the world for the first time. Beautiful was the world, colorful was the world, strange and mysterious was the world! Here was blue, here was yellow, here was green, the sky flowing and the river, the forest rigid and the mountains, everything beautiful, everything full of mystery and magic, and in the midst was he, Siddhartha, awakening, on the path to himself. All of this, all the yellow and blue, river and forest, entered Siddhartha for the first time through his eyes. It was no longer the spell of Mara, no longer the veil of Maya, no longer the meaningless and arbitrary diversity of the phenomenal world that is disdained by the deeply thinking Brahmin, who scorns diversity, who seeks unity. Blue was blue, river was river, and even if in blue and river the singular and the divine were to live hidden within Siddhartha, it was simply the nature and meaning of the divine for here to be yellow, here blue, there sky, there forest, and here Siddhartha. Meaning and essence were not somewhere behind the things, they were within them, within everything.

"How numb and dull I have been!" he thought, walking swiftly on. "If one reads a manuscript, searching for its meaning, one does not scorn the symbols and letters and call them deception, coincidence, worthless hulls. One reads them, studies them, and loves them, letter for letter. I, however, who wanted to read the book of the world and the book of my own essence, I condemned the symbols and letters for the sake of an anticipated meaning. I called the phenomenal world deception, called my eye and my tongue arbitrary and worthless phenomena. No, this is over, I am awakened, I am truly awakened and have not been born until today."

Thinking this thought, Siddhartha stood still once again, suddenly, as though a snake were lying before him on the path.

For suddenly this also became clear to him: he, who truly was like one who has awakened or newly born, he had to begin his life anew from the very beginning. As on this same morning he left the grove Jetavana, the grove of that Sublime One, already awakening, already on the path to himself, it was his intention, and it seemed natural and self-evident to him after his years as an ascetic, to return to his home and his father. But now, and not until this moment in which he stood still as though a snake were lying on his path, he also awakened to this insight: "I am no longer the one I used to be, I am no longer an ascetic, I am no longer a priest, I am no longer a Brahmin. What should I do at home and with my father? Study? Make offerings? Practice meditation? All this is past, all this no longer lies on my path."

Siddhartha stood motionless, and for one moment and one breath his heart froze. He felt it freezing within his chest like a small animal, a bird or a rabbit, as he realized how alone he was. He had been without a home for years and had not felt it. Now he was feeling it. Even in the deepest meditation he had been his father's son, had been a Brahmin, of high caste, a scholar. Now he was only Siddhartha, the awakened one, and nothing more. He drew in his breath deeply and for a moment he froze and shivered. No one was as alone as he. No nobleman who did not belong to the noblemen, no craftsman who did not belong to the craftsmen and found refuge among them, shared their life, spoke their language. No Brahmin who was not among the Brahmins and lived among them, no ascetic who did not find refuge among the Samanas, and even the most forlorn hermit in the forest was not one and alone. Even he was surrounded by belonging, even he belonged to a class that was his home. Govinda had become a monk and thousands of monks were his brothers, wore his clothes, believed in his faith, spoke his language. But he, Siddhartha, where did he belong? Whose life would he share? Whose language would he speak?

From this moment, as the world melted away around him, as he stood alone like a star in the sky, from this moment of cold and trepidation, Siddhartha emerged, more Self than before, more tightly concentrated. He felt that was the last shudder of awakening, the last pain of birth. And at once he walked on, began to walk quickly and impatiently, no longer homeward, no longer to his father, no longer backwards.

PART II

KAMALA

Siddhartha learned new things at every step on his path, for the world was transformed and his heart was enchanted. He saw the sun rising over the wooded mountains and setting over the distant palm shore. He saw the stars arranged in the sky at night and the sickle moon floating like a boat in the blue. He saw trees, stars, animals, clouds, rainbows, cliffs, herbs, flowers, streams, and rivers, the sparkle of dew on the morning shrubs, distant high mountains blue and pale; birds sang and bees, wind blew silvery through the rice paddy. All this, manifold and colorful, had always been there; sun and moon had always shone, rivers had always rushed, and bees had always hummed, but in earlier times for Siddhartha all this had been nothing but a fleeting and deceptive veil before his eyes, beheld with mistrust, destined to be penetrated by thought and destroyed, as it was not essential, as that which was essential lay on the other side of the visible. But now his liberated eye resided on this side, it saw and recognized visibility, sought a home in this world, did not seek the essential, was not aimed at the other side. Beautiful was the world when beheld this way, without seeking, so simple, so

47

childlike. Beautiful were moon and stars, beautiful were stream and bank, forest and cliff, goat and golden beetle, flower and butterfly. Beautiful and sweet it was to go through the world this way, so childlike, so awakened, so open to what was near, so free of mistrust. The sun burned differently on his head, the forest shade cooled differently, stream and cistern tasted differently, squash and banana tasted differently. Short were the days, short the nights, each hour flew quickly away like a sail upon the sea, beneath the sail a ship full of treasures, full of joys. Siddhartha saw a group of monkeys traveling through the high forest canopy, high in the branches, and heard their wild, fervent song. Siddhartha saw a ram pursuing and mating with a sheep. In a reed lake he saw the pike hunting in evening hunger, in front of him the young fish flipped in droves anxiously out of the water, fluttering and sparkling; the scent of strength and fervor emanated from the hasty whirlpools drawn by the determined hunter.

All this had always been there, and he had never seen it; he had not been there. Now he was there, he belonged to it. Light and shadow flowed through his eyes, star and moon flowed through his heart.

Along the way, Siddhartha also remembered all that he had experienced in the garden of Jetavana, the Teaching that he heard there, the divine Buddha, bidding Govinda farewell, the conversation with the Sublime One. He remembered his own words that he had spoken to the Sublime One, every word, and with astonishment he realized that he had said things then that he had not really known at the time. What he said to Gautama—that his, the Buddha's, treasure and secret was not the Teaching, but that which is inexpressible and not teachable, that which he experienced in the hour of his enlightenment— this was just what he was now setting off to experience, what he was now beginning to experience. He had to experience himself now. Of course, for a long time he had already known that his Self was Atman, of the same eternal essence as Brahman. But he had never really found this Self, for he had tried to capture it in the net of thought. Just as the Self was certainly not the body, and not the play of senses, it was also not thought, not the mind, not learned wisdom, not the learned art of drawing conclusions and spinning new thoughts out of old ones. No, even this world of thoughts was still on this side, and no goal could be reached by killing off the arbitrary Self of the senses while fattening the arbitrary Self of thoughts and scholarliness. Both the thoughts as well as the senses were nice things; behind both lay ultimate meaning concealed. Both were to be listened to, both were to be played with, both were neither to be condemned nor overvalued; from both, the secret voices of the innermost core were to be heard. He wanted to strive for nothing other than what the voice instructed him to strive for, to linger nowhere other than where the voice advised. Why had Gautama once, in the hour of hours, sat down beneath the bo tree, where the enlightenment struck him? He had heard a voice, a voice in his own heart, that had instructed him to find rest beneath this tree, and he had not instead chosen self-chastisement, sacrifice, ablution, or prayer, not food or drink, not sleep or dream; he had obeyed the voice. To obey in this way— not external instruction, only the voice—to be prepared in this way, this was good, this was necessary, nothing else was necessary.

During the night, as he slept in the straw hut of a ferryman by the river, Siddhartha had a dream: Govinda stood before him, in a yellow ascetic's robe. Govinda looked sad and asked sadly: "Why have you forsaken me?" Siddhartha then embraced Govinda, flung his arms around him, and as he drew him to his breast and kissed him, it was no longer Govinda but a woman, and from the woman's robe a full breast swelled, at which Siddhartha lay and drank; sweet and strong was the taste of the milk from this breast. It tasted of woman and man, of sun and forest, of animal and flower, of every fruit, of every pleasure. It made one drunk and unconscious.

As Siddhartha awoke, the pale river was shimmering through the door of the hut, and in the forest a dark owl's call sounded, deep and melodious.

When the day began, Siddhartha asked his host, the ferryman, to take him across the river. The ferryman took him across the river on his bamboo raft; the wide expanse of water shimmered red in the morning light.

"This is a beautiful river," he said to his companion.

"Yes," said the ferryman, "a very beautiful river. I love it above all else. I have often listened to it, often looked into its eyes, and I have always learned from it. One can learn a lot from a river."

"I thank you, my benefactor," said Siddhartha as he stepped onto the other bank. "I have no gift to give you, dear friend, and no fare to pay. I am without a home, a Brahmin's son and a Samana."

"I have seen this already," said the ferryman, "and I did not expect a wage from you, and no gift. You will bring the gift another time."

"Do you think so?" said Siddhartha, amused.

"Certainly. This I have also learned from the river: everything returns! You too, Samana, will return. Now farewell! May your friendship be my wage. May you think of me when you are sacrificing to the gods."

Smiling, they parted. Smiling, Siddhartha was pleased about the friendship and friendliness of the ferryman. "He is like Govinda," he thought, smiling. "All the people I meet along the way are like Govinda. All are grateful, although they themselves would be deserving of gratitude. All are submissive, all wish to be a friend, wish to obey, think little. People are children."

Around midday he passed through a village. Before the clay huts, children tumbled around in the alley, played with pumpkin seeds and shells, shouting and scrambling; but they all ran away shyly at the sight of the strange Samana. At the end of the village, the path led through a stream and at the edge of the stream a young woman knelt washing clothes. As Siddhartha greeted her, she raised her head and looked up to him with a smile so that he saw the whites of her eyes flashing. He called a blessing to her, as is the custom among travelers, and asked how much farther the way was to the big city. She then stood up and walked up to him; her moist mouth shimmered beautifully in her young face. She bantered with him, asked whether he had already eaten, and whether it was true that the Samanas slept alone in the forest and were not allowed to have women with them. As she spoke, she placed her left foot on his right one and made a movement that a woman makes when inviting a man to the kind of love-making referred to in the textbooks as "climbing the tree." Siddhartha felt his blood growing warm, and as he remembered his dream at this moment, he bent down slightly to the woman and kissed with his lips the brown tip of her breast. Looking up, he saw her face smiling, full of longing, and the narrowed eyes pleading with desire.

Siddhartha also felt desire and the stirring of his sex, but as he had never touched a woman, he hesitated a moment, while his hands were already eager to reach for her. And at this moment, he heard with a shudder the voice within him, and the voice said, "No." All the magic in the young woman's smiling face then vanished, he saw nothing more than the dewy gaze of a female animal in heat. He stroked her cheek kindly, turned away from her, and disappeared light-footedly before the disappointed woman into the bamboo grove.

On this day, he reached a large city before evening and was happy, for he longed to be among people. He had lived in the forests for years, and the ferryman's straw hut that he had slept in that night was the first roof he had had over his head for a long time.

Just outside the city, by a lovely fenced-in grove, the wanderer encountered a small entourage of servants, loaded with baskets. In their midst, on an ornamented sedan chair carried by four men, seated on red cushions under a colorful canopy, was a woman, the mistress. Siddhartha stopped at the entrance to the pleasure garden and watched the procession, saw the servants, the maids, the baskets, saw the sedan chair, and in the sedan chair he saw the lady. Beneath black hair piled high he saw a very bright, very delicate, very clever face, a light red mouth like a freshly opened fig, eyebrows groomed and drawn in high arches, dark eyes clever and alert, a long pale neck rising from a gown of green and gold, fair hands resting long and slender with wide golden bracelets around the wrists.

Siddhartha saw how beautiful she was and his heart rejoiced. He bowed deeply as the sedan approached, and as he rose he looked into the pale, lovely face, read for a moment in the clever, highly arched eyes, breathed a wisp of scent that he did not know. Smiling, the beautiful woman nodded for a moment and disappeared into the grove with her servants behind her.

This is how I enter this city, thought Siddhartha, under a fair omen! He was tempted to enter the grove at once, but he thought it over and only then did he become aware of how the servants and maids at the entrance had looked at him, how scornfully, how mistrustfully, how dismissively.

I am still a Samana, he thought, still an ascetic and a beggar. I may not stay like this, may not enter the garden like this. And he laughed.

When the next person came along the road he inquired about the grove and the name of the woman, and he learned that this was the grove of Kamala, the famous courtesan, and that aside from the grove, she owned a house in town.

Then he entered the city. He now had a goal.

Pursuing his goal, he let himself be sucked in by the city, he drifted in the current of the streets, stopped in the squares, rested on the stone steps along the river. Toward evening, he befriended a barber's assistant whom he had seen working in the shadow of an archway, whom he found again praying in a temple of Vishnu, to whom he told the stories of Vishnu and Lakshmi. He slept that night by the boats on the river, and early in the morning, before the first customers entered his shop, he had the barber's assistant shave off his beard and cut his hair, comb his hair and rub it with fine oils. Then he went to the river to bathe.

In the late afternoon, as the lovely Kamala approached her grove in her sedan chair, Siddhartha stood at the entrance, bowed, and received the greeting of the courtesan. He then beckoned the servant who was last in the procession and asked him to tell his mistress that a young Brahmin wished to speak with her. After a while, the servant returned, asked the waiting man to follow him, led his follower silently to a pavilion where Kamala lay on a daybed, and left him alone with her.

"Were you not standing outside yesterday and did you not greet me?" asked Kamala.

"Indeed, I saw you yesterday and greeted you."

"But did you not have a beard yesterday, and long hair, and dust in your hair?"

"Truly, you observed correctly, you saw everything. You saw Siddhartha, the Brahmin's son, who left his home to become a Samana, and was a Samana for three years. But now I have left that path and come to this city and the first person I encountered even before I entered the city was you. I have come to tell you this, O Kamala! You are the first woman that Siddhartha has spoken to without lowering his eyes. Never again will I lower my eyes when I encounter a beautiful woman."

Kamala smiled and played with her peacock feather fan, and asked: "Was it only to tell me this that Siddhartha has come?"

"To tell you this, and to thank you for being so beautiful. And if it does not displease you, Kamala, I want to ask you to be my friend and teacher, for I know nothing of the art of which you are a master."

At this Kamala laughed loudly.

"Never has it happened, my friend, that a Samana from the forest has come to me and wanted to learn from me! Never has it happened that a Samana has come to me wearing long hair and an old, torn loincloth. Many youths come to me, and Brahmin's sons are also among them, but they come in nice clothes, they come in fine shoes, they have a pleasant scent in their hair and money in their purses. This, Samana, is what the youths are like who come to me."

Said Siddhartha: "Already I am beginning to learn from you. Yesterday I also learned. I have already removed my beard, have combed my hair, have oil in my hair. Few are the things I am still lacking, excellent lady: fine clothes, fine shoes, money in my purse. Know that Siddhartha has pursued more difficult things than these trivialities and attained them. How could I not achieve what I resolved to do yesterday: to be your friend and learn the pleasures of love from you! You will see that I learn quickly, Kamala, I have learned more difficult things than those you are to teach me. So tell me: Siddhartha does not satisfy you as he is, with oil in his hair but without clothes, without shoes, without money?"

Laughing, Kamala cried out: "No, valued friend, he does not satisfy me yet. He must have clothes, lovely clothes, and shoes, lovely shoes, and lots of money in his purse, and presents for Kamala. Have you understood now, Samana from the forest? Will you remember?"

"Of course I will remember," cried Siddhartha. "How could I forget that which comes from such a mouth! Your mouth is like a freshly opened fig, Kamala. My mouth is also red and fresh, it will match yours, you will see—but tell me, beautiful Kamala, are you not at all afraid of the Samana from the forest who has come to learn love?"

"Why should I be afraid of a Samana, a stupid Samana from the forest, who comes from the jackals and does not yet know at all what a woman is?"

"Oh, he is strong, the Samana, and he fears nothing. He could force you, beautiful girl. He could steal you. He could harm you."

"No, Samana, I have no fear of that. Has a Samana or a Brahmin ever feared that someone could come and seize him and steal his scholarliness, and his devotion, and his pensiveness? No, for they belong to him inherently and he shares of them only what he wishes to share and with whom. It is the same, exactly the same, with Kamala and with the pleasures of love. Beautiful and red is Kamala's mouth, but try to kiss it against Kamala's will and you will receive not a drop of sweetness, although it knows how to give so much sweetness! You learn quickly, Siddhartha, so learn this as well: one can beg for love, buy it, receive it as a gift, find it in the alley, but one cannot steal it. Your thoughts here are misguided. No, it would be a shame if such a handsome youth as yourself were to start off in such a misguided way.

Siddhartha bowed, smiling. "It would be a shame, Kamala, how right you are! It would be a great shame. No, I shall not miss one drop of sweetness from your mouth, nor you the sweetness from mine! It is agreed then: Siddhartha will return when he has what he is still lacking: clothes, shoes, money. But tell me, lovely Kamala, can you not give me one more small piece of advice?"

"Advice? Why not? Who would not like to give advice to a poor, ignorant Samana, who comes from the jackals in the forest?"

"Dear Kamala, then advise me where to go so that I may find these three things most quickly?"

"Many would like to know this, my friend. You must do what you have learned to do and be paid money for it, and clothes, and shoes. There is no other way for a poor man to obtain money. What can you do?"

"I can think. I can wait. I can fast."

"Nothing else?"

"Nothing. Oh yes, I can write poetry. Will you give me a kiss for a poem?"

"I will if I like your poem. What is it called?"

After contemplating for a moment, Siddhartha spoke this verse:

Into her shady grove went the lovely Kamala,
At the grove's gate stood the brown Samana.
Deeply he bowed, as the lotus blossom he saw,
He was thanked by the smiling Kamala.
Sweeter than sacrificing to gods, thought the youth,
Sweeter is sacrificing to the lovely Kamala.

Kamala clapped her hands loudly so that the golden brace-lets jangled.

"Lovely are your verses, brown Samana, and indeed I will lose nothing if I give you a kiss for them."

She drew him to her with her eyes, and he lowered his face to hers and placed his mouth on the mouth that was like a freshly opened fig. For a long time Kamala kissed him, and Siddhartha was deeply astonished at how she taught him how wise she was, how she controlled him, rejected him, allured him, and how this first kiss was followed by a long, well-ordered, well-tested string of kisses, each one different from the others that were still await-ing him. He stood there breathing deeply, and in this moment he was like a child amazed by the abundance of knowledge and things worth learning that opened before his eyes.

"Your verses are very beautiful," cried Kamala. "If I were rich, I would give you pieces of gold for them. But it will be difficult to earn as much money as you need with verses. For you will need a lot of money if you wish to be Kamala's friend."

"How you can kiss, Kamala!" stammered Siddhartha.

"Yes, I can kiss well, and I am therefore not lacking in clothes, shoes, bracelets, and all beautiful things. But what will become of you? Can you do nothing other than think, fast, and write poems?"

"I also know the sacrificial songs," said Siddhartha, "but I do not wish to sing them anymore. I also know incantations, but I do not wish to speak them anymore. I have read the scriptures—"

"Stop," Kamala interrupted. "You can read? And write?"

"Certainly I can. Many people can."

"Most people cannot. Even I cannot. It is very good that you can read and write, very good. The incantations will also be of use to you."

At this moment a servant rushed in and whispered a message in her mistress's ear.

"I have company," cried Kamala. "Hurry and get out of sight, Siddhartha, no one may see you here, remember that! I will see you again tomorrow."

She ordered the maid to give the pious Brahmin a white cloak. Before he knew what was happening, Siddhartha found himself being dragged away by the maid, taken by a roundabout route to a garden house, where he was given a robe, led into the bushes, and urgently advised to find his way out of the grove immediately without being seen.

He did as he was told contentedly. As he was used to the forest, he found his way soundlessly out of the grove and over the hedge. He returned to the city contentedly, carrying the robe rolled up under his arm. In an inn where travelers stop, he stood at the door and begged silently for food, accepted silently a piece of rice cake. Perhaps starting tomorrow, he thought, I will no longer beg anyone for food.

Pride flared up suddenly inside him. He was no longer a Samana, it was no longer befitting of him to beg. He gave the rice cake to a dog and went without food.

"Simple is the life that one leads here in this world," thought Siddhartha. "There are no difficulties. Everything was difficult, arduous, and ultimately hopeless when I was still a Samana. Now everything is light, light like the lessons in kissing that Kamala gives me. I need clothes and money, nothing else, these are small tangible goals that do not disturb one's sleep."

He had long since discovered Kamala's town house; he appeared there the following day.

"It is going well," she called to him. "Kamaswami is expecting you, he is the wealthiest merchant in this city. If he likes you, he will take you into his service. Be clever, brown Samana. I have told him about you through others. Be friendly to him, he is very powerful. But do not be too modest! I do not want you to become his servant, you should become his equal, otherwise I will not be satisfied with you. Kamaswami is beginning to grow old and idle. If he likes you, he will place a lot of trust in you."

Siddhartha thanked her and laughed, and when she learned that he had eaten nothing that day or the day before, she ordered bread and fruit to be brought and served him.

"You've been lucky," she said on parting. "One door after the other is opening before you. Why is this? Do you have magic power?"

Siddhartha said: "Yesterday I told you that I know how to think, to wait, and to fast, but you found this to be useless.

But it is very useful, Kamala, you will see. You will see that the stupid Samanas from the forest are able to learn and do many fine things that you cannot. The day before yesterday I was still a ragged beggar, yesterday I kissed Kamala, and soon I will be a merchant and have money and all the things that you value."

"Well, yes," she conceded. "But where would you be without me? What would you be if Kamala were not helping you?"

"Dear Kamala," said Siddhartha and stood up his full height, "when I came to you in your grove, I was taking the first step. It was my resolve to learn love from this most beautiful woman. From the moment I made this resolve, I also knew that I would carry it out. I knew that you would help me; with your first glance at the grove's entrance, I already knew."

"And if I had not been willing?"

"You were willing. You see, Kamala: if you throw a stone into the water, it takes the fastest path to the bottom. This is how it is when Siddhartha has a goal, a resolution. Siddhartha does nothing, he waits, he thinks, he fasts, but he passes through the things of the world like a stone through water, without doing anything, without moving; he is drawn, he lets himself fall. His goal draws him, for he allows nothing to enter his soul that could contend with this goal. This is what Siddhartha learned among the Samanas. It is what fools call magic and what they think is induced by demons. Nothing is induced by demons, there are no demons. Anyone can perform magic, anyone can reach his goals if he can think, if he can wait, if he can fast."

Kamala listened to him. She loved his voice, she loved the look in his eye.

"Maybe it is as you say, my friend," she said softly. "Maybe it is also because Siddhartha is a handsome man, because women like the look in his eye, that good luck comes to him."

With a kiss, Siddhartha said farewell. "May it be so, my teacher. May my look always please you, may good luck always come from you to me!"

AMONG THE CHILD-PEOPLE

Siddhartha went to see the merchant Kamaswami. He was shown into a rich house, servants led him between valuable tapestries to a chamber in which he awaited the master of the house.

Kamaswami entered, a swift, sleek man with heavily graying hair, with very clever, cautious eyes, with a covetous mouth. Master and guest exchanged friendly greetings.

"I have been told," began the merchant, "that you are a Brahmin, a scholar, but are seeking to enter the service of a merchant. Are you in need, Brahmin, that you are seeking such service?"

"No," said Siddhartha, "I am not in need and have never been in need. You see, I come from the Samanas, among whom I lived for a long time."

"If you come from the Samanas, how can you not be in need? Are the Samanas not entirely without possessions?"

"I am without possessions," said Siddhartha, "if that is what you mean. I certainly am without possessions. But I am so voluntarily, so I am not in need."

"But what do you intend to live on, if you are without possessions?"

"I have never thought of that, sir. I have been without possessions for more than three years and have never thought about what to live on."

"You have lived from the possessions of others."

"Presumably this is so. The merchant also lives from the wealth of others."

"Well said. But the merchant does not take from others for free; he gives them his wares in return."

"Indeed, this appears to be the way it is. Everyone takes, everyone gives, such is life."

"But, if you will permit, what do you intend to give if you are without possessions?"

"Everyone gives what he has. The warrior gives strength, the merchant gives wares, the teacher teachings, the farmer rice, the fisher fish."

"Very well. And what is it then that you have to give? What is it that you have learned, that you can do?

"I can think. I can wait. I can fast."

"Is that all?"

"I think that it *is* all!"

"And what use is it? Fasting, for example—what good is it?"

"It is very good, sir. When a person has nothing to eat, fasting is the cleverest thing he can do. If, for example, Siddhartha had not learned to fast, he would have to take on any service on this very day, with you or someone else, for hunger would force him to do so. As it is, Siddhartha can wait calmly, he knows no impatience, he knows no distress, hunger may besiege him for a long time and he can laugh at it. This, sir, is what fasting is good for."

"You are right, Samana. Wait a moment."

Kamaswami went out and returned with a scroll that he handed to his guest, asking: "Can you read this?"

Siddhartha looked at the scroll, on which a bill of sale had been written, and began to read its contents aloud.

"Excellent," said Kamaswami. "And would you write something on this paper for me?"

He gave him paper and a pen, and Siddhartha wrote and returned the paper.

Kamaswami read: "Writing is good, thinking is better. Cleverness is good, patience is better."

"You can write beautifully," praised the merchant. "We still have many things to discuss with one another. For today, please be my guest and take residence in this house."

Siddhartha thanked him and accepted, and took up residence in the tradesman's house. Clothing was brought to him, and shoes, and a servant prepared his daily bath. A lavish meal was served twice a day, but Siddhartha ate only once a day and neither ate meat nor drank wine. Kamaswami told him about his business, showed him wares and storerooms, showed him accounts. Siddhartha learned many new things, listened a lot, and spoke little. And mindful of Kamala's words, he never subordinated himself to the merchant, forced him to treat him as his equal, indeed even more than his equal. Kamaswami operated his business with dedication and often with passion.

Siddhartha, however, saw it all as a game whose rules he was striving to learn exactly, but whose substance did not touch his heart.

He had not been in Kamaswami's house for long before he began to take part in his host's trade. Daily, however, at the hour she named, he visited the beautiful Kamala, in lovely clothes and fine shoes, and soon he also brought her gifts. Her red, clever mouth taught him many things. Her delicate, agile hand taught him many things. He—who in matters of love was still a boy and tended to plunge himself blindly and insatiably into pleasure as into an abyss—he was taught from the beginning that one cannot receive pleasure without giving pleasure, and that every gesture, every caress, every touch, every glance, every tiny place on the body has its mystery, which, when awoken, brings happiness to the knowledgeable. She taught him that lovers may not part after celebrating their love without each first admiring the other, without each being as much conquered as conqueror, so that neither becomes afflicted by gluttony and boredom and the terrible feeling of having abused or having been abused. He spent wonderful hours with the beautiful and clever artist, became her pupil, her lover, her friend. Here with Kamala lay the value and meaning of his present life, not in Kamaswami's trade.

The merchant entrusted him with the composition of important letters and contracts and became accustomed to consulting him on all important matters. He soon saw that while Siddhartha knew little of rice and wool, of shipping and trade, he had good intuition and Siddhartha surpassed him, the merchant, in calmness and composure, and in the art of being able to listen to and to see beneath the surface of other people. "This Brahmin," he said to a friend, "is not a real merchant and will never become one, his soul is never passionate when we do business. But he possesses the secret of those to whom success comes on its own, whether he was born under a lucky star, whether it is magic, whether it is something that he learned among the Samanas. He always seems only to be playing with the business dealings, they never really sink into him, they never dominate him, he never fears failure, he is never troubled by loss."

The friend advised the tradesman: "Give him a third of the profit for the business he negotiates for you, but also let him bear the same portion of the losses when losses occur. This will make him more eager."

Kamaswami followed this advice. Siddhartha, however, did not concern himself with it much. If he made a profit, then he accepted it indifferently; if he made a loss, he laughed and said: "Oh look, so this time it went badly!"

Indeed, it seemed that he had no interest in business. Once he traveled to a village to purchase a large rice harvest. When he arrived, however, the rice had already been sold to another tradesman. Despite this, Siddhartha remained in this village for several days, gave a feast for the farmers, gave the children copper coins, celebrated a wedding, and returned very content from the journey. Kamaswami reproached him for not returning immediately, for wasting time and money. Siddhartha replied: "Stop scolding, dear friend! Nothing has ever been achieved by scolding. If a loss has been made, let me bear the loss. I am very pleased with this journey. I met many different kinds of people, a Brahmin became my friend, children rode on my knee, farmers showed me their fields, no one took me for a tradesman."

"This is all very lovely," cried Kamaswami indignantly, "but you are in fact a tradesman, I should say! Or did you travel solely for your own pleasure?"

"Certainly," laughed Siddhartha, "certainly I traveled for my own pleasure. Why else? I got to know people and regions, I enjoyed kindness and trust, I found friendship. You see, dear friend, had I been Kamaswami, I would have turned back full of anger and haste the moment I saw my purchase foiled, and time and money would indeed have been wasted. As it was, however, I had good days, learned, experienced joy, harmed neither myself nor others with anger and hastiness. And if I ever return there, perhaps to purchase a later harvest or for whatever other purpose, the kind people will give me a kind and cheerful welcome, and I will praise myself for not having shown haste and resentment. So let it be, my friend, and do not harm yourself by scolding! When the day comes when you see that this Siddhartha is bringing you harm, say the word and Siddhartha will be on his way. Until then, however, let us be content with one another."

In vain were also the merchant's attempts to convince Siddhartha that he was eating his—Kamaswami's—bread. Siddhartha ate his own bread, or rather they both ate the bread of others, everyone's bread. Siddhartha never lent an ear to Kamaswami's worries, and Kamaswami had many worries. If a deal in progress threatened to fail, if a shipment seemed to be lost, if a debtor seemed unable to pay, Kamaswami could never convince his partner that is it useful to speak words of distress or anger, to have a wrinkled brow, to sleep poorly. When Kamaswami once confronted him, claiming that he had learned everything that he knew from him, he answered: "Please do not mock me with such jokes! From you I have learned how much a basket of fish costs and how much interest one can request for borrowed money. These are your areas of knowledge. I did not learn to think from you, dear Kamaswami; you should rather seek to learn it from me."

Indeed, his soul was not in the trading. The business was good for bringing in money for Kamala, and he brought in much more than he needed. Otherwise, Siddhartha's sympathy and curiosity lay only with the people whose trading, crafts, worries, amusements, and follies had previously been as foreign and far away as the moon. As easy as it was for him to speak to everyone, live with everyone, learn from everyone, he was just as aware that there was something that separated him from the others, and this something was his time as a Samana. He saw the people living their lives in a childlike or animal way that he both loved and despised. He saw them laboring, saw them suffering and turning gray about things that seemed to him entirely unworthy of this price; for money, for small pleasures, for small honors, he saw them scolding and insulting one another, he saw them lamenting pain that a Samana smiles at and suffering from deprivations that a Samana does not feel.

He was open to everything that these people brought him. Welcome was the tradesman who offered to sell him linen, welcome was the indebted man seeking a loan, welcome was the beggar who took an hour to tell him the story of his poverty, and who was not half as poor as any Samana. He treated the wealthy foreign tradesman no differently than the servant who shaved him, and the street vendor whom he allowed to cheat him of small change when buying bananas. When Kamaswami came to him to bemoan his troubles or to reproach him on account of business dealings, he listened curiously and cheerfully, was amazed by him, tried to understand him, conceded to him a little, just the amount that seemed necessary to him, and turned away from him toward the next one who sought his attention. And many came to him, many to trade with him, many to cheat him, many to sound him out, many to appeal to his compassion, many to hear his advice. He gave advice, he commiserated, he gave presents, he let himself be cheated a bit, and this whole game and the passion with which all people play this game occupied his thoughts just as much as the gods and Brahman had once occupied them.

At times he felt, deep within his breast, a dying, faint voice that warned faintly, lamented faintly, so that he could barely hear it. He would then become aware for an hour that he was leading a strange life, that the things he was doing were nothing but a game, that he was indeed cheerful and felt joy at times, but that real life was nevertheless flowing past him and not touching him. Like a juggler juggling his balls, he played with his business dealings, with the people around him, watched them, found amusement in them; with his heart, with the source of his being, he did not take part. The source flowed somewhere, as if far away from him, flowed and flowed invisibly, had nothing more to do with his life. And several times he was startled by such thoughts and wished that he too could be allowed to participate with passion and with his heart in all the day's childlike activities, to truly live, to truly act, to truly enjoy, and to live instead of only standing by as a spectator. But he always returned to the beautiful Kamala, learned the art of love, practiced the cult of pleasure in which, more than anywhere else, giving and receiving become one. He chatted with her, learned from her, gave her advice, received advice. She understood him better than Govinda had once understood him, she was more similar.

Once he said to her: "You are like me, you are different from most people. You are Kamala, nothing else, and within you there is a stillness and refuge that you can enter at any time and be at home within yourself, just as I can. Few people have this, and yet all could have it."

"Not all people are clever," said Kamala.

"No," said Siddhartha, "that is not the reason. Kamaswami is just as clever as I am and still has no refuge within himself. Others have it although they have the intelligence of small children. Most people, Kamala, are like a falling leaf that drifts and twists itself through the air, and staggers, and tumbles to the ground. Others, however, a very few, are like stars who travel a fixed path, no wind reaches them, they carry their law and their path within themselves. Among all the scholars and

Samanas, of which I have known many, was one of this kind, a perfect one—never can I forget him. It is Gautama, the Sublime One, the teacher of that doctrine. A thousand disciples hear his teaching every day, follow his direction every hour, but they are all falling leaves, they do not carry doctrine and law within themselves."

Kamala looked at him with a smile. "Again you are speaking of him," she said. "Again you are having Samana thoughts."

Siddhartha was silent, and they played the game of love, one of the thirty or forty different games that Kamala knew. Her body was as supple as that of a jaguar and a hunter's bow; he who had learned love from her was adept at many pleasures, many secrets. For a long time she played with Siddhartha, lured him, refused him, forced him, enveloped him: rejoiced in his mastery until he was vanquished and lay exhausted at her side.

The hetaera leaned over him, gazed for a long time at his face, into his eyes that had grown so weary.

"You are the best lover," she said pensively, "that I have seen. You are stronger than others, more agile, more willing. You have learned my art well, Siddhartha. One day, when I am older, I wish to bear your child. But you have still remained a Samana, my dear, still you do not love me, you love no one. Is it not so?"

"It may be so," said Siddhartha wearily. "I am like you. You do not love either—how could you practice love as an art otherwise? Perhaps people of our kind cannot love. The child-people can: that is their secret."

SANSARA

For a long time Siddhartha had lived the life of the world and its pleasures without belonging to it. His senses, which he had suffocated during his fervid Samana years, had awoken again. He had tasted wealth, had tasted lust, had tasted power, yet he had remained a Samana in his heart for a long time, as Kamala, the clever one, had correctly recognized. Still, it was the art of thinking, of waiting, of fasting that steered his life; still the people of the world, the child-people, remained foreign to him, as he was foreign to them.

The years ran by. Shrouded in well-being, Siddhartha barely felt their passing. He had grown rich, he long since owned his own house and servants, and a garden outside of town by the river. People liked him, they came to him when they needed money or advice, but no one was close to him except Kamala.

That noble, bright awakeness that he had once experienced, at the height of his youth, in the days following Gautama's sermon, after parting from Govinda, that tense anticipation, that proud standing alone without teachings and without teachers, that lithe readiness to hear the divine voice in his own heart, had gradually become memory, had become ephemeral; distant and faint flowed the holy spring that had once been near, that once had flowed within himself. To be sure, much of that which he had learned from the Samanas, which he had learned from Gautama, which he had learned from his father, the Brahmin, had remained within him for a long time: moderate living, pleasure in thought, hours of meditation, secret knowledge of the Self, of his eternal being that is neither body nor consciousness. Much of this had remained within him, but one after another had sunk to the bottom and covered itself with dust. Just as the potter's wheel, once set in motion, continues to spin for a long time and only slowly tires and comes to rest, so too had the wheel of asceticism, the wheel of thinking, the wheel of differentiation in Siddhartha's soul continued to spin for a long time, was still spinning, but it spun slowly and hesitantly and was close to a standstill. Slowly, as moisture seeps into the dying tree stump, slowly filling it and making it rot, the world and lethargy had seeped into Siddhartha's soul, slowly filled his soul, made it heavy, made it tired, lulled it to sleep. In return, his senses had come to life, they had learned many things, experienced many things.

Siddhartha had learned to trade, to wield power over people, to take pleasure with a woman; he had learned to wear nice clothes, to give orders to servants, to bathe himself in fragrant waters. He had learned to eat delicately and carefully prepared dishes, also fish, also meat and fowl, spices and sweets, and to drink the wine that makes one lethargic and forgetful. He had learned to play with dice and upon a chessboard, to watch the dancing girls, to have himself carried in a sedan chair, to sleep in a soft bed. But still he felt that he was different from the others and superior to them; he had always watched them with a touch of mockery, with a touch of mocking contempt, with the very same contempt that a Samana always feels for the worldly people. When Kamaswami was sickly, when he was annoyed, when he felt offended, when he was plagued by his merchant woes, Siddhartha had always observed it with mockery. Only slowly and imperceptibly, with the passing of harvests and monsoons, had his mockery grown more weary, had his superiority become more silent. Only slowly, among his growing riches, had Siddhartha himself taken on some characteristics of the child-people, some of their childlike and their fearful manners. And yet he envied them, envied them all the more the more similar to them he became. He envied them for the one thing that he lacked and they possessed, for the importance that they were able to attach to their lives, for the passion of their joys and fears, for the anxious yet sweet happiness of their eternal infatuation. With themselves, with women, with their children, with honor or money, with plans or hopes—these people were constantly infatuated. But this he had not learned from them, not this, this child's joy and child's folly; all he learned from them were the unpleasant things, which he himself despised. It happened more and more often that he would remain lying in bed for a long time the morning after a festive evening and feel dull and tired. It happened that he would become annoyed and impatient when Kamaswami bored him with his worries. It happened that he laughed all too loudly when he lost a game of dice. His face was still more clever and more spiritual than others, but it laughed seldom, and one after the other it took on the traits so often found in the faces of rich people, those traits of discontentedness, of sickliness, of displeasure, of lethargy, of unkindness. Slowly he was stricken by the rich man's illness of the soul.

Like a veil, like a thin fog, weariness descended upon Siddhartha, slowly, every day a bit thicker, every month a bit hazier, every year a bit heavier. Like a new garment that with time grows old—that with time loses its lovely color, becomes stained, becomes wrinkled and battered at the seams, and here and there begins to show weak, threadbare patches—Siddhar-tha's new life that began after parting from Govinda had also grown old, had lost color and sheen, had collected wrinkles and stains; and hidden beneath the surface, already hideously peeking out here and there, waited disappointment and disgust. Siddhartha did not notice it. He only noticed that the bright and certain inner voice that had once awoken within him and guided him again and again during his luminous times had become silent.

The world had captured him; pleasure, lustfulness, leth-argy, and in the end even that which he found to be the most foolish vice and despised and derided above all: greed. Property, ownership, and wealth had also captured him in the end, were no longer games and trinkets, had become chain and burden. It was a strange and devious path that led Siddhartha to fall into this final and most vile dependency: dice playing. From that moment at which he ceased to be a Samana in his heart,

Siddhartha had begun to gamble for money and valuables—a custom of the child-people that he usually took part in with a smile and light heart—with increasing anger and passion. He was a feared player, his bets were so high and brazen that few dared to challenge him. He played the game out of his heart's distress; the loss and squandering of the wretched money brought him an angry pleasure; in no other way could he show his contempt for wealth, the idol of the merchants, more clearly and derisively. And so he bet high and ruthlessly, hating himself, deriding himself, won thousands, threw thousands away, lost money, lost jewelry, lost a country house, won again, lost again. That fear, that horrible and oppressive fear that he felt while rolling the dice, while worrying about high bets—he loved that fear and constantly sought to renew it, to increase it, to stimulate it higher and higher, for in this feeling alone was he still able to feel something like happiness, something like inebriation, something like exalted life in the midst of his sated, dull, insipid life.

And after every great loss he sought new wealth, pursued trade more fervently, forced his debtors to pay more strictly, for he wanted to continue playing, he wanted to continue squandering, to continue showing wealth his contempt. Siddhartha lost his composure when suffering losses, he lost his patience with defaulters, lost his good nature with beggars, lost his desire to give away and lend his money to supplicants. He who laughed as he lost ten thousand at one roll of the dice became increasingly intolerant and petty in his business dealings; at night he sometimes dreamed of money! And every time he awoke from this ugly enchantment, every time he saw that his face in the mirror on the bedroom wall had grown more aged and ugly, every time shame and disgust assailed him, he fled further, fled to a new gamble, fled to the numbness of lust, of wine, and from there back to the urge of accumulating and acquiring. In this senseless cycle, he ran himself tired, ran himself old, ran himself sick.

Then one day he was warned by a dream. He had spent the evening hours with Kamala in her beautiful pleasure garden. They had sat beneath the trees, in conversation, and Kamala had spoken pensive words, words behind which sorrow and weariness lay hidden. She had asked him to tell her about Gautama and could not hear enough about him, how pure his eyes, how still and beautiful his mouth, how kind his smile, how peaceful his gait had been. For a long time he had had to talk about the sublime Buddha and Kamala had sighed and said: "One day, perhaps soon, I too will follow this Buddha. I will give him my pleasure garden and take my refuge in his Teaching." But then she had aroused him and bound him to her in love play with painful fervor, amid bites and tears, as though she were trying to squeeze the last sweet drop out of this vain, ephemeral pleasure. Never had it become so strangely clear to Siddhartha how closely related lust is to death. Then he had lain at her side with Kamala's face close to him, and beneath her eyes and beside the corners of her mouth he had read, clearly as never before, an anxious script, a script of fine lines, of quiet furrows, a script reminiscent of autumn and old age, like Siddhartha himself who, only in his forties, had already noticed gray hairs here and there among the black. Weariness was written on Kamala's beautiful face, weariness from traveling a long path that had no cheerful end, weariness and the first signs of wilting, and secret, still unspoken, perhaps even still unknown, trepidation: fear of old age, fear of autumn, fear of having to die. Sighing, he took leave of her, his soul full of reluctance and full of secret trepidation.

Then Siddhartha had spent the night in his house with dancing girls and wine, had played the superior one among the others of his standing, which he no longer was, had drunk a lot of wine and long after midnight had gone to bed, weary but still agitated, close to tears and despair. For a long time he had sought sleep in vain, his heart full of a misery that he thought he could no longer bear, full of a disgust that he felt had permeated him like the tepid, vile taste of the wine, the all-too-sweet, tedious music, the all-too-soft smiles of the dancing girls, the all-too-sweet perfume of their hair and breasts. More than anything else, however, he disgusted himself, his perfumed hair, the smell of wine from his mouth, the flaccid fatigue and aversion of his skin. Like one who has had far too much to eat or drink, vomits it up again in agony, and yet is glad for the relief, so did the sleepless man, in an immense surge of disgust, wish to rid himself of these pleasures, these habits, this whole senseless life and himself. Only with the first light of day and the awakening of the first bustling on the street in front of his town house did he fall asleep, did he find a few moments of half numbness, a hint of sleep. During these moments he had a dream:

Kamala kept a rare little songbird in a golden cage. He dreamed of this bird. He dreamed that this bird, which always sang at dawn, had become silent, and as he noticed this he went over to the cage and looked inside: there the little bird was dead and lay stiff on the bottom. He took it out, weighed it for a moment in his hand, and then threw it away, out into the alley, and at the same moment he was terribly startled and his heart pained him, as if by throwing away this dead bird he had cast from him all that was valuable and good.

Waking from this dream with a start, he felt himself surrounded by deep sadness. Worthless, it seemed to him, worthless and senseless was the life he had led; nothing living, nothing in any way precious or worth keeping had remained in his hands. Alone he stood and empty, like a castaway on the shore.

Somberly Siddhartha betook himself to a pleasure garden that belonged to him, locked the gate, sat down beneath a mango tree, felt death in his heart and horror in his breast, sat and felt himself dying within, wilting within, coming to an end. Gradually he gathered his thoughts and traveled his entire life's path once more in his mind, from the first days he could remember. When had he ever experienced happiness, felt true bliss? Oh yes, he had many times. He had tasted it in his boyhood years when he won the praise of the Brahmins, when he, far ahead of others his age, had excelled at reciting the holy verses, at debating with the scholars, in assisting at the sacrifices. Then he had felt in his heart: "A path lies before you to which you have been called, the gods are waiting for you." And again as a youth, as the goal of all contemplation, which soared higher and higher, had torn him up and out of his flock of fellow strivers, as he grappled in pain with the meaning of Brahman, as all insight attained only sparked new thirst within him, there again, in the midst of thirst, in the midst of pain, he had felt it: "Onward! Onward! You have a calling!" He had heard this voice when he left his home and chose the life of a Samana, and again when he left the Samanas for the Perfect One, and also when he left him to venture into the unknown. How long it had been since he had heard that voice, how long had he failed to reach any heights, how flat and dull was the path that he had been following for many long years, without high goals, without thirst, without exaltation, contenting himself with small pleasures yet never being satisfied! All these years, he had, without knowing it, been attempting and yearning to become a person like these many people, like these children, and in doing so his life had become much poorer and more miserable than theirs, for their goals were not his, nor were their worries; the entire world of the Kamaswami-people had only been a game to him, after all, a dance that one watches, a comedy. Only Kamala was dear to him, had been valuable to him—but was she still? Did he still need her, or she him? Were they not playing a game without an end? Was it necessary to live for that? No, it was not necessary! This game was called Sansara, a game for children, a game that may be lovely to play once, twice, ten times—but again and again?

Siddhartha knew then that the game was over, that he could no longer play it. A shudder ran through his body; within him, he felt that something had died.

That entire day he sat under the mango tree thinking of his father, thinking of Govinda, thinking of Gautama. Did he have to leave them to become a Kamaswami? He was still sitting when night had descended. As he looked up to see the stars, he thought: "Here I sit under my mango tree, in my pleasure garden." He smiled a little—was it even necessary, was it right, was it not a foolish game that he owned a mango tree, that he owned a garden?

He put this behind him as well, this also died within him. He rose, took leave of the mango tree, took leave of the pleasure garden. As he had gone without food all day, he felt an intense hunger and thought of his house in town, of his chamber and bed, of the table with food. He smiled wearily, shook himself, and took leave of these things.

In the same night hour Siddhartha left his garden, left the city, and never returned. For a long time Kamaswami had him searched for, as he believed he had fallen into robbers' hands. Kamala sent no one to search for him. When she heard that Siddhartha had disappeared she was not surprised. Had she not always expected it? Was he not a Samana, a man without a home, a pilgrim? She had felt this most strongly during their last meeting, and in the midst of the pain of her loss she was glad that she had drawn him so vehemently to her heart this last time, that she had felt so entirely possessed and permeated by him one last time.

When she received the first news of Siddhartha's disappearance, she went to the window where she held a rare songbird captive in a golden cage. She opened the door of the cage, took the bird out, and let it fly. For a long time she looked after it, the flying bird. From that day on, she received no more visitors and kept her house closed. After some time, however, she became aware that from the last encounter with Siddhartha she was now pregnant.

BY THE RIVER

Siddhartha wandered through the forest, already far from the city, and knew nothing other than that he could no longer go back, that this life as he had been leading it for many years was over and done with, savored and sucked dry to the point of disgust. Dead was the songbird of which he had dreamt. Dead was the bird in his heart. Deep was his entanglement in Sansara; he had soaked up disgust and death from all sides like a sponge soaks up water until it is full. Full of tedium he was, full of misery, full of death; there was nothing left in the world that could allure him, please him, console him.

He longed to know nothing more of himself, to have peace, to be dead. If only lightning would come and strike him dead! If only a tiger would come and devour him! If only there were a wine, a poison to numb him, to bring him oblivion and sleep, and no more awakening! Was there any filth with which he had not yet defiled himself, a sin or folly that he had not committed, a bleakness of the soul with which he had not burdened himself? Was it even still possible to live? Was it possible to draw breath over and over again, to exhale, to feel hunger, to eat

again, to sleep again, to lie with a woman again? Was this cycle not exhausted for him and concluded?

Siddhartha reached the great river in the forest, the same river across which a ferryman had once taken him when he was still a young man coming from Gautama's city. At this river he came to a stop, remained standing hesitantly on its bank. Fatigue and hunger had weakened him, and why should he continue—where to, toward which goal? No, there were no more goals, there was nothing other than the deep, painful desire to shake off this whole desolate dream, to spit out this stale wine, to put an end to this wretched and disgraceful life.

Over the riverbank hung a bowed tree, a coconut tree. Siddhartha leaned against its trunk with his shoulder, lay his arm around the trunk, and looked down into the green water that flowed and flowed beneath him, looked down and found himself filled entirely with the desire to let himself go and sink in this water. A dreadful emptiness was reflected back to him from the water that was answered by the terrible emptiness within his soul. Yes, he had reached the end. There was nothing left for him but to extinguish himself, to shatter the failed construct of his life, to throw it away, at the feet of the gods who mocked him. This was the great purge that he had been longing for: death, shattering the form that he hated! May the fish devour him, this dog Siddhartha, this madman, this foul and rotten body, this limp and abused soul! May the fish and crocodiles devour him, may the demons tear him to pieces!

With his face contorted he stared into the water, saw his face mirrored, and spit at it. With deep weariness he released

his arm from the tree trunk and turned slightly to let himself fall down vertically, to finally go under. He sank, with closed eyes, toward death.

Then a sound flickered from remote regions of his soul, from past times in his weary life. It was a word, a syllable that he muttered to himself without thoughts in slurred speech, the old opening and closing word of all Brahmin prayers, the holy Om, meaning something like "Perfect One" or "Perfection." And the moment that the sound Om touched his ear, his dormant spirit awoke suddenly and recognized the foolishness of his actions.

Siddhartha was deeply startled. So this was the state he was in, so lost was he, so adrift and abandoned by all knowledge that he could have sought death, that this wish, this child's wish could have grown within him: to find peace by extinguishing his body! That which all the torment of recent times, all disenchantment, all desperation had not achieved was achieved by this moment at which the Om pierced his consciousness: he recognized himself in his misery and delusion.

"Om!" he muttered to himself: "Om!" And knew about Brahma, knew about the indestructibility of life, knew again about all things divine that he had forgotten.

But this was only a moment, a flash. At the foot of the coconut tree, Siddhartha sank down, laid his head on the root of the tree, and sunk into a deep sleep.

Deep was his sleep and free of dreams: it had been a long time since he had known such sleep. When he awoke after some hours, it seemed to him that ten years had passed; he heard the quiet flowing of the water, did not know where he was and who had brought him here, opened his eyes, saw with astonishment trees and sky above him, and remembered where he was and how he had come here. But this took him a long time and the past seemed to him to be concealed by a veil, infinitely distant, infinitely far away, infinitely indifferent. He knew only that his former life (during the first moment of reflection, this former life seemed to him to be a previous incarnation from the distant past, like an early prebirth of his present self) was now abandoned, that he, in his disgust and misery, had even wanted to throw his life away, but that he had regained consciousness by a river, beneath a coconut tree, the holy word Om on his lips, had then fallen asleep and upon awakening, now beheld the world as a new man. Softly he murmured to himself the word Om to which he had fallen asleep, and his entire long sleep seemed to him to have been nothing but one long, immersed Om chanting, an Om thinking, a submersion and complete immersion into Om, into that which is nameless, perfect.

What a wonderful sleep it had been! Never had a sleep refreshed him, renewed him, rejuvenated him in this way! Had he perhaps really died, gone down, and been reborn in a new shape? But no, he recognized himself, he recognized his hand and his feet, recognized the place where he lay, recognized this self within his breast, this Siddhartha, the willful one, the strange one, but this Siddhartha was nonetheless transformed, was renewed, was oddly well rested, oddly awake, joyful, and curious.

Siddhartha rose up and saw that he was sitting across from a man, a stranger, a monk in a yellow robe with a shaved head, in the position of contemplation. He observed the man, who had neither hair on his head nor a beard, and he had not observed him for long before he recognized in this monk Govinda, the friend of his youth, Govinda, who had taken his refuge with the sublime Buddha. Govinda had aged, too, but his face still carried the old features; it spoke of diligence, of faithfulness, of searching, of apprehension. But when Govinda, feeling his gaze, opened his eyes and looked at him, Siddhartha saw that Govinda did not recognize him. Govinda was pleased to find him awake; apparently he had been sitting here for a long time waiting for him to awaken, although he did not know him.

"I was asleep," said Siddhartha. "How did you get here?"

"You were asleep," answered Govinda. "It is not good to sleep in places where there are often snakes and the animals of the forest have their paths. I, sir, am a disciple of the sublime Gautama, the Buddha, the Sakyamuni, and was on a pilgrimage along this path with a number of our disciples when I saw you lying and sleeping in a place where it is dangerous to sleep. I therefore tried to wake you, O sir, and when I saw that your sleep was very deep I stayed behind the other disciples and sat with you. And then, so it seems, I fell asleep myself, I who wanted to watch over your sleep. I have performed my duty poorly, tiredness overcame me. But now that you are awake, let me go so that I may catch up with my brothers."

"I thank you, Samana, for guarding my sleep," Siddhartha said. "Kind are the disciples of the Sublime One. Now you may go."

"I am going, sir. May you always find yourself well."

"I thank you, Samana."

Govinda made the sign of greeting and said: "Farewell."

"Farewell, Govinda," said Siddhartha.

The monk stood still.

"Forgive me, sir, how do you know my name?"

Siddhartha then smiled.

"I know you, O Govinda, from your father's hut, and from the Brahmin school, and from that hour in the grove of Jetavana when you took your refuge with the Sublime One."

"You are Siddhartha!" Govinda cried out. "Now I recognize you and do not understand how I could have failed to recognize you at once. Welcome, Siddhartha, great is my pleasure to see you again."

"I, too, am pleased to see you again. You were the guardian of my sleep, thank you again for this, although I would have needed no guardian. Where are you going, O friend?"

"I am going nowhere. We monks are always traveling, so long as it is not monsoon season, we always move from place to place, live according to the rule, proclaim the Teaching, take alms, move on. Always it is so. But you, Siddhartha, where are you going?"

Said Siddhartha: "It is the same with me, friend, as with you. I am going nowhere. I am only traveling. I am on a pilgrimage."

Govinda said: "You say you are on a pilgrimage and I believe you. But forgive me, O Siddhartha, you do not look like a pilgrim. You are wearing the dress of the wealthy, you are wearing the shoes of a nobleman, and your hair smells of fragrant water, not the hair of a pilgrim, not the hair of a Samana."

"Indeed, dear friend, you have observed well, your sharp eye sees everything. But I did not say to you that I am a Samana. I am on a pilgrimage. And so is it: I am on a pilgrimage."

"You are on a pilgrimage," said Govinda. "But few people pilgrim in such clothing, few in such shoes, few with such hair. Never, in my many years of pilgrimage, have I met such a pilgrim."

"I believe you, my Govinda. But now, today, you have met just such a pilgrim, in such shoes, with such a garment. Remember, dear friend: ephemeral is the world of shapes, ephemeral, highly ephemeral are our clothes and the style of our hair, and our hair and bodies themselves. I wear the clothes of a rich man, you have seen this correctly. I wear them because I was a rich man, and wear my hair like the worldly people and sensualists because I was one of them."

"And now, Siddhartha, what are you now?"

"I do not know, I know it as little as you do. I am traveling. I was a rich man and am one no longer; and what I will be tomorrow, I do not know."

"You have lost your wealth?"

"I have lost it, or it has lost me. It has gone astray. The wheel of shapes turns quickly, Govinda. Where is the Brahmin Siddhartha? Where is the Samana Siddhartha? Where is the rich man Siddhartha? The ephemeral changes quickly, Govinda, this you know."

Govinda looked at the friend of his youth for a long time, his eyes full of doubt. Then he took leave of him the way one takes leave of a nobleman and went on his way.

With a smiling face Siddhartha watched after him, he loved him still, this faithful one, this apprehensive one. And how, in this moment, in this glorious hour after his wonderful sleep, permeated by Om, could he not love anyone or anything! Precisely therein lay the enchantment that had taken place within him during sleep and through the Om: that he loved everything, that he was filled with joyful love for all that he saw. And precisely thereon, so it seemed to him now, had he been so ill before that he could have loved nothing and no one.

With a smiling face Siddhartha watched after the monk as he walked away. The sleep had strengthened him greatly, but great was the torment of hunger, for he had eaten nothing for two days and the time when he had been hardened to hunger was long past. With anguish, yet also with laughter, he thought of this time. Then, he recalled, he had boasted to Kamala of three things, he had been capable of three noble and unassailable arts: fasting—waiting—thinking. These had been his possessions, his power and strength, his solid staff; in the diligent, arduous years of his youth he had learned these three arts, nothing else. And now they had abandoned him, not one of them remained his, not fasting, not waiting, not thinking. For the most miserable things had he had sacrificed them, for the most ephemeral, for sensual pleasure, for luxury, for wealth! Strange indeed had it turned out for him. And now, it seemed, now he had truly become one of the child-people.

Siddhartha thought about his situation. It was hard for him to think, he didn't really feel like it, but he forced himself.

Now that all these most ephemeral things have slipped away from me again, he thought, now I am standing under the sun again as I once stood as a small child, I own nothing, I know nothing, I can do nothing, I have learned nothing. How curious this is! Now, when I am no longer young, when my hair is already half gray, when my strength is subsiding, now I am starting again from the beginning, from childhood! Again he had to smile. Yes, strange was his fate! Things were going downhill with him, and now he was once more standing empty and naked and stupid in the world. But he could not feel sorrowful about this, no, indeed he felt a great urge to laugh, to laugh at himself, to laugh at this strange, foolish world.

"Things are going downhill with you!" he said to himself with a laugh, and as he said this his gaze fell upon the river, and he also saw the river going downhill, always wandering downhill, and singing and being cheerful as it went. This pleased him indeed, he gave the river a friendly smile. Was this not the river in which he had wanted to drown himself, once, one hundred years ago, or had this been a dream?

Curious indeed was my life, he thought, curious are the detours it has taken. As a boy, I was only concerned with gods and sacrifices. As a youth, I was only concerned with asceticism, with thinking and meditation, was searching for Brahman, venerated the eternal in Atman. But as a young man, I followed the penitents, lived in the forest, suffered heat and frost, learned to starve, taught my body to die away. Wonderful it was when insight then came to me in the Teaching of the great Buddha; I felt knowledge of the oneness of the world circulating within me like my own blood. But I also had to take leave of Buddha and the great knowledge. I went and learned with Kamala the pleasure of love, learned with Kamaswami to trade, amassed money, squandered money, learned to love my stomach, learned to please my senses. It took me many years to lose my spirit, to unlearn thinking, to forget oneness. Is it not as if I were slowly and with great detours turning from a man into a child, from a thinker into one of the child-people? And still this path has been very good, and still the bird in my breast has not died. But what a path it was! I have had to go through so much foolishness, through so much vice, through so much error, through so much disgust and disillusionment and lamentation just to become a child again and be able to start anew. But this was right, my heart says yes to it, my eyes laugh at it. I had to experience despair, I had to sink down to the most foolish of all thoughts, to the thought of suicide, to be able to experience grace, to hear Om again, to be able to truly sleep and truly awaken again. I had to become a fool to find Atman within myself again. I had to sin to be able to live again. Where else may my path be leading me? Foolish it is, this path, it goes in loops, perhaps it goes in circles. May it go as it will, I will follow it.

Wonderfully he felt joy welling in his breast.

Where, he asked his heart, where did you get this joyfulness? Might it come from this long, good sleep that has done me so much good? Or from the word Om that I spoke? Or because I have escaped, because my flight is accomplished, because I am finally free again and stand like a child under the sky? Oh how good it is to have fled, to have become free! How pure and beautiful the air is here, how good to breathe! There, in the place I have run from, there everything smelled of salve, of spices, of wine, of excess, of lethargy. How I hated that world of the rich, of gluttons, of gamblers! How I hated myself for having remained in that dreadful world for so long! How I hated myself, robbed myself, poisoned, tormented, made myself old and wicked! No, never again will I believe, as I once so enjoyed believing, that Siddhartha is wise! But this I have done well, this pleases me, this I must praise: that an end has now come to all hatred for myself, to that foolish and bleak life! I praise you, Siddhartha, after so many years of foolishness, you had another idea, you did something, you heard the bird singing in your breast and followed it!

Thus he praised himself, was pleased with himself, listening with curiosity to his stomach, which was growling with hunger. He felt that he had completely tasted and spit out a piece of suffering, a piece of misery, in these past times and days—devoured it to the point of despair and death. This was good. He could have stayed with Kamaswami for much longer, earning money, squandering money, fattening his belly, and letting his soul die of thirst; he could have stayed living in that soft, well-cushioned hell if this had not come: the moment of complete bleakness and despair, that utmost moment when he was hanging above the flowing water and had been ready to destroy himself. That he had felt this despair, this deepest disgust, and that he had not succumbed to it, that the bird, the happy source and voice within him was still alive after all, this was why he felt this joy, this was why he laughed, this was why his face gleamed beneath his grayed hair.

"It is good," he thought, "to taste for oneself everything that one needs to know. I learned already as a child that worldly desires and wealth are not good things. I have known it for a long time, I have only experienced it now. And now I know it, know it not only with my memory but also with my eyes, with my heart, with my stomach. Good for me that I know it!"

For a long time he pondered his transformation, listened to the bird as it sang for joy. Had this bird not died within him, had he not felt its death? No, something else had died within him, something that had long since been yearning to die. Was it not that which he had once, in his fervent penitent years, wanted to kill? Was it not his Self, his small, scared, and proud Self that he had fought with for so many years, that had defeated him again and again, that reemerged after each killing, forbidding joy, feeling fear? Was it not this that had finally found its death today, here in the forest by this lovely river? Was it not because of this death that he was now like a child, so full of trust, so devoid of fear, so full of joy?

Now Siddhartha also sensed why he, as a Brahmin, as a penitent, had fought with this Self in vain. Too much knowledge had hindered him, too many holy verses, too many rules of sacrifice, too much castigation, too much acting and striving! Full of pride he had been, always the cleverest, always the most eager, always one step ahead of everyone, always the knowing one and spiritual one, always the priest or wise man. Into this priestliness, into this pride, into this spirituality his Self had crawled, and here it sat firmly and grew while he thought he was killing it with fasting and penitence. Now he saw it, and saw that the secret voice had been right, that no teacher would ever have been able to deliver him. This is why he had had to go out into the world, to lose himself to pleasure and power, to women and money; had had to become a tradesman, a gambler, a drinker, and greedy man until the priest and Samana within him were dead. This is why he had had to continue enduring these ugly years, to endure the disgust, the emptiness, the senselessness of a bleak and forlorn life, to the end, to bitter despair, until even Siddhartha the sensualist, Siddhartha the greedy man could die. He had died, a new Siddhartha had awoken from sleep. He too would grow old, he too would have to die one day; ephemeral was Siddhartha, ephemeral was every shape. But today he was young, was a child, the new Siddhartha, and was full of joy.

He thought these thoughts, listened to his stomach with a smile, listened gratefully to a buzzing bee. Cheerfully he looked into the flowing river, never had a body of water pleased him as much as this one, never had he heard the voice and allegory of moving water so strongly and beautifully. It seemed to him that the river had something special to say, something that he did not yet know, that was still awaiting him. In this river, Siddhartha had wanted to drown, and in it the old, weary, despairing Siddhartha had drowned today. The new Siddhartha, however, felt a deep love for this flowing water and resolved not to leave it again so soon.

THE FERRYMAN

By this river is where I wish to stay, thought Siddhartha. It is the same one that I once crossed on the way to the child-people. A friendly ferryman guided me then—to him is where I wish to go. From his hut is where my path once led me to a new life that has now grown old and died—may my present path, my present new life find its beginnings there as well!

Affectionately he gazed into the flowing water, into the transparent green, into the crystalline lines of its mysterious design. He saw bright pearls rising from the depths, silent bubbles swimming on the surface, sky blue reflected in it. With a thousand eyes, the river gazed at him, with green, with white, with crystalline, with sky blue. How he loved this water, how it delighted him, how grateful he was to it! In his heart he heard the voice speaking, the newly awakened one, and it said to him: "Love this water! Stay with it! Learn from it!" Oh yes, he wanted to learn from it, he wanted to listen to it. He who understood this water and its mysteries, it seemed to him, he would also understand many other things, many mysteries, all mysteries.

But of all the river's mysteries, he saw only one today, which captured his soul. He saw that this water flowed and flowed, always it flowed, and still it was always there, was always and forever the same and still new at every moment! Oh, who could grasp this, who could understand? He could not understand and grasp it, he felt only an inkling stirring, distant memory, divine voices.

Siddhartha arose; the flurry of hunger in his body was becoming unbearable. Acquiescent, he wandered on, up the riverbank path, against the current, listening to the current, listening to the growling hunger in his body.

When he reached the ferry, the same boat lay waiting and the same ferryman who had once taken the young Samana across the river stood in the boat. Siddhartha recognized him. He, too, had aged greatly.

"Will you ferry me across?" he asked.

The ferryman, amazed to see such a noble man wandering alone and by foot, took him into the boat and pushed off.

"What a lovely life you have chosen," spoke the guest. "It must be lovely to live every day by this water and to travel upon it."

Smiling, the oarsman swayed: "It is lovely, sir, it is as you say. But is not every life, is not every work lovely?"

"That may be. But I envy you for yours."

"Oh, you would soon lose your pleasure in it. This is nothing for people in fine clothes."

Siddhartha laughed. "I have already been regarded with distrust once today on account of my clothes. Ferryman, would you not accept these clothes, which are a burden to me? For you must know, I have no money with which to pay your fare."

"The gentleman is jesting," laughed the ferryman.

"I am not jesting, my friend. You see, once before you ferried me across this water in your boat out of charity. Do so again today and accept my clothes in exchange."

"And does the gentleman wish to travel on without clothes?"

"Oh, I would like not to travel on at all. Most of all, ferryman, I would like you to give me an old breech cloth and keep me on as your assistant, or rather as your apprentice, for I must first learn how to handle the boat."

For a long time the ferryman looked at the stranger, searching.

"Now I recognize you," he said at last. "You slept in my hut once, it was a long time ago, surely it must have been more than twenty years ago, and I ferried you across the river and we took leave of one another as good friends. Were you not a Samana? I can no longer recall your name."

"My name is Siddhartha and I was a Samana when you last saw me."

"Then welcome, Siddhartha. My name is Vasudeva. You will, I hope, be my guest today as well and sleep in my hut and tell me where you are coming from and why your fine clothes are such a burden to you."

They had arrived at the middle of the river and Vasudeva leaned into the oar more heavily to cope with the current. He worked calmly, his eye on the tip of the boat, with strong arms. Siddhartha sat and watched him, and remembered how even then, on that final day of his time as a Samana, love for this man had stirred in his heart. Gratefully he accepted Vasudeva's invitation. When they landed on the bank, he helped him to tie the boat to the posts, and then the ferryman asked him to enter the hut, offered him bread and water, and Siddhartha ate with pleasure, and also ate with pleasure of the mango fruits that Vasudeva offered him.

Thereafter, with the sun nearly setting, they sat on a tree trunk by the riverbank and Siddhartha told the ferryman of his origins and his life, as he had seen it today, in that hour of despair, passing before his eyes. His story continued deep into the night.

Vasudeva listened with great attentiveness. He took in everything as he listened, origin and childhood, all the learning, all the seeking, all joy, all suffering. Among the ferryman's virtues, this was one of the greatest: he knew as few others do how to listen. Without saying a word, the speaker could sense how Vasudeva let the words sink in, still, open, waiting, how he lost not a single one, expected not a single one with impatience, assigned neither praise nor blame, only listened. Siddhartha felt what a joy it was to confide in such a listener, to sink his own life, his own seeking, his own suffering into his heart.

Toward the end of Siddhartha's story, however, as he spoke of the tree by the river and of his deep fall, of the holy Om, and how after his slumber he felt such a love for the river, the ferryman listened with doubled attentiveness, utterly and completely absorbed, with closed eyes.

But when Siddhartha was silent and a long silence had passed, then Vasudeva said: "It is as I thought. The river has spoken to you. It is also a friend to you, it also speaks to you. That is good, that is very good. Stay with me, Siddhartha, my friend. I once had a wife, her bed was next to mine, but she has long since died, I have lived alone for a long time. Now you shall live with me, there is room and food for us both."

"I thank you," said Siddhartha. "I thank you and accept. And I also thank you, Vasudeva, for listening to me so well! Rare are the people who know how to listen. And I have never met one who can listen as well as you. Herein I shall also learn from you."

"You shall learn it," said Vasudeva, "but not from me. The river taught me to listen, it will teach you as well. It knows everything, the river, one can learn everything from it. You see, you have already learned this from water that it is good to strive downwards, to sink, to seek the depths. The rich and noble Siddhartha is to become a rower, the learned Brahmin Siddhartha is to become a ferryman: this you have also been told by the river. You will also learn the other thing from it."

Siddhartha spoke after a long pause: "Which other thing, Vasudeva?"

Vasudeva arose. "It has grown late," he said, "let us go to sleep. I can't tell you what the other thing is, my friend. You will learn it, perhaps you know it already. You see, I am not a scholar, I do not know how to speak, nor do I know how to think. I only know how to listen and be pious; I have learned nothing else. If I could say and teach it, then perhaps I would be a wise man, but as it is I am only a ferryman and it is my task to ferry people across the river. I have ferried many across, thousands, and for all of them my river has been nothing other than a hindrance on their journeys. They traveled for money and business, to weddings and to pilgrimages, and the river was in their way, and the ferryman was there to carry them over the hindrance quickly. For a few among the thousands, however, a small few, four or five, the river had ceased to be a hindrance; they heard its voice, they listened to it, and the river became holy to them, as it is holy to me. Let us retire now, Siddhartha."

Siddhartha stayed with the ferryman and learned to handle the boat, and when there was nothing to do at the ferry, he worked with Vasudeva in the rice paddy, gathered wood, picked the fruits of the pisang trees. He learned to build an oar, and learned to mend the boat, and to weave baskets, and was happy about everything that he learned, and the days and months went by quickly. But more than Vasudeva could teach him was that which the river taught him. From it he learned incessantly. Above all, he learned from it how to listen, to listen with a still heart, with a waiting, opened soul, without passion, without desire, without judgment, without opinion.

He lived beside Vasudeva in friendship, and from time to time they exchanged words with one another, few and long contemplated words. Vasudeva was no friend of words; Siddhartha rarely succeeded in moving him to speak.

"Have you," he asked him once, "have you also learned this secret from the river: that time does not exist?"

A bright smile spread across Vasudeva's face.

"Yes, Siddhartha," he said. "Is it not this that you mean: that the river is everywhere at once, at its source and its estuary, at the waterfall, at the ferry, at the rapids, in the sea, in the mountains, everywhere at once, and that for it there is only the present, not the shadow of the future?"

"That is it," said Siddhartha. "And when I had learned this, I looked at my life and it was also a river, and the boy Siddhartha was separated from the grown Siddhartha and the aged Siddhartha only by shadows, not by anything real. Siddhartha's previous births were also not the past, and his death and his return to Brahman not the future. Nothing was, nothing will be; everything is, everything has being and presence."

Siddhartha spoke with delight, deep was his pleasure at this enlightenment. Oh, was not then all suffering time, was not all being in agony and being afraid time? Would not all that is heavy, all that is hostile in the world be gone and overcome as soon as one had overcome time, as soon as one had thought away time? With delight he had spoken, but Vasudeva simply smiled at him brightly and nodded affirmation, nodded silently, ran his hand over Siddhartha's shoulder, turned back to his work.

And once again, during the monsoon season when the river was swollen and rushed powerfully, then Siddhartha said: "Is it not true, my friend, that the river has many voices, very many voices? Does it not have the voice of a king, and a warrior, and a bull, and a nocturnal bird, and a woman giving birth, and one sighing, and a thousand other voices?"

"This is so," nodded Vasudeva. "All creatures' voices are in its voice."

"And do you know," Siddhartha continued, "which word it speaks when you succeed in hearing all its ten thousand voices at once?"

Vasudeva's face laughed happily, he leaned toward Siddhartha and spoke the holy Om into his ear. And this was just what Siddhartha had also heard.

And with each time, his smile became more similar to that of the ferryman, became nearly just as bright, nearly just as imbued with happiness, just as luminous from a thousand small wrinkles, just as childlike, just as aged. Many travelers, seeing the two ferrymen together, took them for brothers. They often sat together in the evening on the riverbank on the tree trunk in silence and listened to the water, which for them was not water but the voice of life, the voice of Being, of eternally Becoming. And it happened from time to time that both would think of the same things while listening to the river, of a conversation from the day before yesterday, of one of their travelers whose face and fortune occupied their minds, of death, of their childhood, and at that same moment when the river had told them something good, they would both look at one another, both thinking exactly the same thing, both pleased with the same answer to the same question.

Something emanated from the ferry and from the two ferrymen that was felt by some of the travelers. It happened from time to time that a traveler, after he had looked into one of the ferrymen's faces, began to tell of his life, told of suffering, confessed to bad deeds, asked for solace and counsel. It happened from time to time that someone requested permission to spend an evening with them so as to listen to the river. It also happened that curious people came who had been told that this ferry was inhabited by two wise men, or magicians, or saints. The curious people asked many questions, but they received no answers, and they found neither magicians nor wise men, they found only two old, friendly little men who seemed to be mute and somewhat peculiar and dim-witted. And the curious people laughed and conversed about how foolishly and gullibly the people spread such empty rumors.

The years passed by and no one counted them. Then one day monks came pilgriming along, followers of Gautama, the Buddha, and they requested to be ferried across the river, and from them the ferrymen learned that they were traveling back to their great teacher as quickly as possible, for the news had been spread that the Sublime One was gravely ill and would soon die his final human death so as to enter into salvation. Not long afterwards, another group of monks came pilgriming, and then another, and the monks as well as most of the other travelers and wanderers spoke of nothing but Gautama and his imminent death. And just as people stream from all around and all directions for a military campaign or the crowning of a king and gather in colonies like ants, so they now streamed as though drawn by magic to the place where the great Buddha awaited his death, where this tremendous event was to occur and the great man of an age, the Perfect One, was to enter into glory.

Siddhartha thought often during this time of the dying wise man, the great teacher, whose voice had warned nations and awoken hundreds of thousands, whose voice he too had once heard, whose holy face he too had once beheld with awe. Affectionately, he commemorated him, saw his path to perfection before him, and remembered with a smile the words that he as a young man had once addressed to him, the Sublime One. They had, it seemed to him, been proud and precocious words; he remembered them with a smile. He had long since known that he was no longer separated from Gautama, whose Teachings he had not been able to accept. No, no teaching could be accepted by a true seeker, one who truly wants to find. But one who has found could approve of each and every teaching, every path, every goal; he was no longer separated from all the thousands of others who lived in the Eternal, who breathed the Divine.

On one of these days when so many were pilgriming to the dying Buddha, Kamala, once the most beautiful of the courtesans, was also among the pilgrims. She had long since withdrawn from her former life, had given her garden to Gautama's monks, had taken refuge in his Teaching, counted herself among the friends and patronesses of the pilgrims. Together with the boy Siddhartha, her son, she had set forth on foot, in simple dress, upon hearing the news that Gautama's death was near. She was traveling along the river with her little son; but the boy had soon grown tired, wanted to go home, wanted to rest, wanted to eat, became stubborn and tearful.

Kamala had to rest with him often, he was accustomed to having his way, she had to feed him, had to console him, had to scold him. He did not understand why he had to go on this difficult, sad pilgrimage with his mother, to an unfamiliar place, to a strange man, who was holy and who lay dying. Let him die, what concern was this to the boy?

The pilgrims were not far from Vasudeva's ferry when little Siddhartha once again forced his mother to rest. She herself, Kamala, had grown tired, and while the boy chewed on a banana, she crouched down on the ground, closed her eyes a little, and rested. But suddenly she let out a wailing cry, the boy looked at her in fright and saw her face pale with horror, and from beneath her dress escaped the small black snake that had bitten Kamala.

Urgently they both now walked down the path to get to where people were and arrived near the ferry, where Kamala sunk to the ground and was not able to go any farther. But the boy began to cry out miserably, kissing and embracing his mother in between cries, and she too joined in his loud cries for help until the sounds reached Vasudeva's ear, who was standing by the ferry. Quickly he came running, took the woman in his arms, carried her to the boat; the boy ran alongside, and soon they all arrived in the hut where Siddhartha stood at the hearth, making a fire. He looked up and saw the face of the boy first, which was strangely familiar, reminding him of things long forgotten. Then he saw Kamala, whom he recognized at once although she was lying unconscious in the arms of the ferryman, and then he knew that it was his own son whose face had reminded him so strongly, and his heart stirred in his breast.

Kamala's wound was washed, but it was already black and her body swollen. Medicine was poured between her lips. Her consciousness returned. She lay on Siddhartha's bed in the hut, and bent over her stood Siddhartha, who had once loved her so deeply. It seemed to her to be a dream. She gazed into her friend's face smiling; only slowly did she become aware of her situation, remember the bite, call anxiously for the boy.

"He is with you, do not worry," said Siddhartha.

Kamala looked into his eyes. She spoke with a heavy tongue, benumbed by the poison. "You have grown old, my dear," she said, "you have grown gray. But you resemble the young Samana who once came into my garden without clothes and with dusty feet. You resemble him much more closely than you did then, when you left me and Kamaswami. In your eyes you resemble him, Siddhartha. Oh, I have also grown old— did you even recognize me?"

Siddhartha smiled: "I recognized you at once, Kamala, my dear."

Kamala nodded toward her boy and said: "Did you recognize him as well? He is your son."

Her eyes wandered and fell shut. The boy cried. Siddhartha took him on his knee, let him cry, stroked his hair, and at the sight of the child's face he recalled a Brahmin prayer that he had once learned when he himself was a little boy. Slowly, in a singing voice, he began to speak it, the words came flowing back to him from his past and his childhood. And with his singsong, the boy became calm, whimpered every now and then, and fell asleep. Siddhartha laid him on Vasudeva's bed. Vasudeva stood at the hearth and cooked rice. Siddhartha threw him a glance, which he returned smiling.

"She will die," said Siddhartha quietly.

Vasudeva nodded, the firelight from the hearth passed across his friendly face.

Again Kamala regained consciousness. Pain distorted her face, Siddhartha's eyes read the suffering on her lips, on her pallid cheeks. He read it silently, attentively, waiting, immersed in her suffering. Kamala could feel it, her gaze sought his eye.

Looking at him she said: "Now I see that also your eyes have changed. They have become much different. But how do I still recognize that you are Siddhartha? It is you, and it is not you."

Siddhartha did not speak, silently his eyes looked into hers.

"Have you attained it?" she asked. "Have you found peace?"

He smiled and laid his hand on hers.

"I see it," she said, "I see it. I too will find peace."

"You have found it," spoke Siddhartha in a whisper.

Kamala gazed into his eyes unwaveringly. She thought about how she had wanted to make a pilgrimage to Gautama to see the face of the Perfect One, to breathe his peace, and that instead of this she had found Siddhartha, and that it was good, just as good as if she had seen Gautama. She wanted to tell him this, but her tongue no longer obeyed her will. She looked at him in silence, and he saw in her eyes the life extinguish. When the final pain had filled her eyes and broken, when the final shudder had run down her limbs, his finger closed her lids.

For a long time he sat and looked at her lifeless face. For a long time he beheld her mouth, her old, tired mouth whose lips had grown thin, and remembered that he once, in the spring of his years, had compared this mouth to a freshly opened fig.

For a long time he sat, read the pale face, the tired wrinkles, filled himself with the sight, saw his own face lying just the same way, just as white, just as extinguished, and saw at the same time his face and hers young, with the red lips, with the burning eyes, and the feeling of the presence and simultaneity permeated him completely, the feeling of eternity. He felt deeply, more deeply than ever before in this hour, the indestructibility of every life, the eternity of every moment.

When he stood up, Vasudeva had prepared rice for him. But Siddhartha did not eat. In the shed where their goat stood, the two old men arranged straw for themselves and Vasudeva lay down to sleep. Siddhartha, however, went outside and spent the night sitting in front of the hut, listening to the river, with the past washing around him, touched and enfolded by all the ages of his life at once. From time to time, however, he would rise, walk to the door of the hut, and listen to make sure the boy was asleep.

Early in the morning, before the sun could be seen, Vasudeva came out of the shed and walked up to his friend.

"You did not sleep," he said.

"No, Vasudeva. I sat here, I listened to the river. It told me many things, it filled me deeply with the healing thought, with the thought of oneness."

"You have experienced sorrow, Siddhartha, but I see that no sadness has entered your heart."

"No, dear friend, how could I be sad? I, who was rich and happy, have now become even richer and happier. My son has been given to me."

"I, too, welcome your son. But now, Siddhartha, let us set to work, there is much to do. The same bed on which Kamala died is where my wife once died. The same hill on which I once built my wife's funeral pyre is where we shall build Kamala's funeral pyre."

While the boy slept, they built the funeral pyre.

THE SON

Shy and weeping, the boy had attended his mother's funeral; somber and shy, he had listened to Siddhartha, who greeted him as his son and welcomed him in Vasudeva's hut. Pallid, he sat for days on the burial hill, refused to eat, locked his eyes, locked his heart, resisting and refusing fate.

Siddhartha was gentle with him, and let him be, and honored his grief. Siddhartha understood that his son did not know him, that he could not love him as a father. Slowly, he also saw and understood that the eleven-year-old was spoiled, a mother's boy, and that he had grown up in the customs of wealth, accustomed to fine meals, a soft bed, accustomed to commanding servants. Siddhartha understood that this grieving, spoiled boy could not be suddenly and compliantly content in a strange place and in poverty. He did not force him, he completed many tasks for him, always chose the best morsels for him. Slowly, he hoped to win him over, with friendly patience.

Rich and happy he had called himself when the boy came to him. As time flowed by, however, and the boy remained distant and somber, as he revealed a proud and defiant heart, refused to work, showed no reverence for his elders, stole from Vasudeva's fruit trees, Siddhartha began to understand that it was not happiness and peace that had come to him with his son but sorrow and worry. But he loved him and preferred the sorrow and worry of love to the happiness and joy of his life without the boy. Since the young Siddhartha's arrival in the hut, the old men had divided their work. Vasudeva had taken over the ferryman's duties again and Siddhartha, in order to be with his son, had taken over the duties in the hut and field.

For a long time, for long months, Siddhartha waited for his son to understand him, for him to accept his love, for him to perhaps return it. For long months, Vasudeva, watching, waited and remained silent. One day, as the young Siddhartha had once again tormented his father with defiance and moods and broken both rice bowls, Vasudeva took his friend aside in the evening and spoke with him.

"Forgive me," he said, "I speak to you with a friendly heart. I can see that you are struggling, I can see that you are troubled. Your son, dear friend, is causing you worry, and he is causing me worry as well. The young bird is accustomed to a different life, a different nest. Unlike you, he did not run away from wealth and the city in disgust and aversion; he had to leave all this behind against his will. I asked the river, my friend, many times I have asked it. But the river laughs, it laughs at me, laughs at me and you, and shakes with laughter at our foolishness. Water seeks water, youth seeks youth, your son is not in a place where he can flourish. Ask the river as well, hear its answer as well!"

Distressed, Siddhartha looked into his friendly face, in whose many wrinkles constant cheerfulness resided.

"How can I part from him?" he said quietly, ashamed. "Give me more time, dear friend! You see, I am fighting for him, I am trying to win his heart, with love and with friendly patience I wish to capture it. The river shall also speak to him one day, he also has a calling."

Vasudeva's smile blossomed more warmly. "Oh yes, he also has a calling, he also is of eternal life. But do we know, you and I, what his calling is, to which path, to which deeds, to which suffering? His suffering will not be slight, for his heart is proud and hard; such hearts must suffer a lot, make many mistakes, do much wrong, burden themselves with much sin. Tell me, dear friend: Do you discipline your son? Do you force him? Do you strike him? Do you punish him?"

"No, Vasudeva, I do none of these things."

"I knew it. You do not force him, do not strike him, do not command him because you know that soft is stronger than hard, water stronger than rock, love stronger than violence. Very good, I praise you. But is it not a mistake for you to believe that you do not force him, do not punish him? Do you not bind him in bands with your love? Do you not shame him daily and make things yet more difficult for him with your kindness and patience? Do you not force him, the proud and spoiled boy, to live in a hut with two old banana eaters, for whom even rice is a delicacy, whose thoughts cannot be his, whose hearts are old and still and beat differently from his? Is he not coerced by all this, not punished?"

Troubled, Siddhartha looked at the ground. Quietly he asked: "What do you think I should do?"

Said Vasudeva: "Take him to the city, take him to his mother's house; there will still be servants there, give him to them. And if no one is left, take him to a teacher, not to be taught, but so that he will be among other boys and girls and in the world that is his. Have you never thought of this?"

"You have seen into my heart," said Siddhartha sadly. "Often I have thought of this. But you see, how can I send him, who already lacks a gentle heart, into that world? Will he not become lavish, will he not lose himself to pleasure and power, will he not repeat all his father's errors, will he not perhaps become lost in Sansara altogether?"

The ferryman's smile shone brightly; he touched Siddhartha's arm gently and said: "Ask the river about it, my friend! Hear it laugh about it! Do you really believe that you have committed your follies to spare your son from committing them? And are you even capable of protecting your son from Sansara? How? Through teaching, through prayer, through admonition? My friend, have you forgotten that story entirely, that instructive story of the Brahmin's son Siddhartha, that you once told me here on this spot? Who protected the Samana Siddhartha from Sansara, from sin, from greed, from folly? Was his father's piety, his teacher's admonition, was his own knowledge, his own searching able to protect him? Which father, which teacher could have protected him from living his life himself, staining himself with life, burdening himself with guilt, drinking the bitter drink himself, finding his path himself? Do you believe,

SIDDHARTHA

my friend, that anyone might be spared this path? Perhaps your
little son, because you love him, because you would like to spare
him sorrow and pain and disappointment? But even if you were
to die ten times for him, you would not be able to relieve him
of the smallest part of his destiny."

Never before had Vasudeva spoken so many words. Siddhartha thanked him kindly; full of worry he went into the hut,
and for a long time he could find no sleep. Vasudeva had not
told him anything that he had not already thought or known.
But it was knowledge that he could not act on; more powerful
than the knowledge was his love for the boy, more powerful was
his affection, his fear of losing him. Had he ever lost his heart
so completely to anything before, had he ever loved another
person so much, so blindly, so painfully, so failingly, and yet so
happily?

Siddhartha could not follow his friend's advice, he could
not give up his son. He let his son order him about, he let him
disrespect him. He remained quiet and waited, commenc-
ing daily the silent battle of friendliness, the soundless war of
patience. Vasudeva also remained quiet and waited, with kindness, wisdom, forbearance. In patience they were both masters.

Once, when the boy's face reminded him very much of
Kamala, Siddhartha suddenly remembered words that Kamala
had once said to him ages ago, in the days of youth. "You cannot
love," she had said to him, and he had agreed, and compared
himself to a star and the child-people to falling leaves, and still
he had also felt a reproach in these words. Indeed, he never
had been able to lose himself entirely and surrender himself

to another person, to forget himself, to commit follies of love for the sake of another; he had never been able to do so and this, it seemed to him at the time, had been the great difference separating him from the child people. But now, since his son had arrived, now he, Siddhartha, had also fully become a child-person, suffering because of another person, loving another person, lost to love, a fool because of love. Now he too felt, belatedly, this strongest and strangest of passions in his life, suffered because of it, suffered miserably, and yet he was blissful, yet he was somewhat renewed, was somewhat richer.

Of course he sensed that this love, this blind love for his son, was a passion, something very human, that it was Sansara, a muddy spring, a dark water. But at the same time he felt that it was not worthless, that it was necessary, that it came out of his own being. This pleasure also wanted to be atoned for, this pain also wanted to be tasted, these follies also committed.

Meanwhile the son let him commit his follies, let him pursue him, let him humble himself daily before his moods. This father had nothing that could have delighted him and nothing that he would have feared. He was a good man, this father, a good, kind, gentle man, perhaps a very pious man, perhaps a saint—none of these were attributes that could have won the boy's heart. Boring was this father who held him captive in his miserable hut, boring was he who answered all bad behavior with a smile, all insults with friendliness, all spite with kindness—this was the old deceiver's most hated trick. The boy would much rather have been threatened by him, mistreated by him.

There came a day when the young Siddhartha's thoughts reached a breaking point and he turned openly against his father. His father had given him a task, he had bid him to gather brushwood. But the boy did not leave the hut, he remained standing there, defiant and angry, stamped on the floor, balled his fists, and in a violent outburst he shouted hatred and contempt into his father's face.

"Get the brushwood yourself!" he cried, seething, "I am not your servant. I know that you will not strike me, you wouldn't dare; I know that you want to constantly punish me and belittle me with your piety and forbearance. You want me to become like you, just as pious, just as gentle, just as wise! But I—mark my words!—I would rather become a thief and murderer to spite you and go to hell rather than become like you! I hate you, you are not my father, even if you were my mother's lover ten times over!"

Anger and grief overflowed within him, seethed in a hundred harsh and vicious words toward his father. Then the boy ran away and did not return until late in the evening.

But the next morning, he was gone. Gone too was a small basket woven of two-colored bast in which the ferrymen kept the copper and silver coins that they received as fare. Gone too was the boat; Siddhartha saw it lying on the opposite bank. The boy had run away.

"I must follow him," said Siddhartha, who had been trembling with misery since the boy's revilement the day before. "A child cannot walk through the forest alone. He will die. We must build a raft, Vasudeva, to cross the water."

"We will build a raft," said Vasudeva, "to retrieve our boat, which the boy has stolen. But you should let the boy go, my friend, he is no longer a child, he can fend for himself. He is looking for the way to the city and he is right, don't forget. He is doing what you failed to do. He is taking care of himself, he is following his course. O Siddhartha, I see that you are suffering, but you are suffering from pain that one wants to laugh at, that you will soon laugh at."

Siddhartha did not answer. He was already holding the ax in his hands, and began to build a raft of bamboo, and Vasudeva helped him to bind the stalks together with grass ropes. Then they crossed to the other side, drifted far downstream, pulled the raft upstream along the opposite riverbank.

"Why did you bring the ax?" asked Siddhartha.

Vasudeva said: "It may be that our boat's oar has been lost."

But Siddhartha knew what his friend was thinking. He was thinking that the boy would have thrown away or broken the oar to avenge himself and keep them from following him. And indeed, there was no longer an oar in the boat. Vasudeva pointed to the bottom of the boat and looked at his friend with a smile as if to say, "Don't you see what your son is trying to tell you? Don't you see that he does not wish to be followed?" But he did not say this with words. He set about making a new oar. Siddhartha, however, took leave in order to search for the runaway. Vasudeva did not hinder him.

Siddhartha had been walking in the forest for a long time when the thought came to him that his searching was futile. Either the boy was far ahead of him, he thought, and had already reached the city, or, if he were still on his way, he would hide from him, the one pursuing him. As he thought further, he also found that he was not worried about his son, that in his innermost he knew that he had not died nor was he in danger in the forest. Still, he ran without resting, no longer to rescue him, just out of longing, just to see him again. And he ran until just before the city.

When he reached the wide road near the city, he stopped at the entrance to the beautiful pleasure garden that once belonged to Kamala, where he once saw her, in the sedan chair, for the first time. That which had once been arose again in his soul, again he saw himself standing there, young, a bearded, naked Samana, with hair full of dust. Siddhartha stood for a long time and looked through the open gate into the garden; he saw monks in yellow robes walking beneath the beautiful trees.

For a long time he stood thinking, seeing images, listening to the story of his life. For a long time he stood, looked at the monks, saw instead of them the young Siddhartha, saw the young Kamala walking under the tall trees. Distinctly he saw himself, as he was served by Kamala, as he received her first kiss, as he proudly and scornfully looked back on his life as a Brahmin, as he proudly and longingly began his worldly life. He saw Kamaswami, saw the servants, the feasts, the dice players, the musicians, saw Kamala's songbird in the cage, lived all this again, breathed Sansara, was old and weary again, felt the disgust again, felt the desire again to extinguish himself, recovered again by way of the holy Om.

After he had stood at the gate to the garden for a long time, Siddhartha realized that the longing that had driven him to this place was foolish, that he could not help his son, that he was not allowed to cling to him. Deeply he felt the love for the runaway boy in his heart—like a wound—and felt at the same time that the wound had not been given to him so that he would wallow in it, that it must become a blossom and shine.

That the wound was not yet blossoming, did not yet shine, made him sad. In place of the desired goal, which had driven him here in pursuit of his runaway son, was now emptiness. Sadly he sat down, felt something in his heart dying, felt emptiness, saw no more joy, no goal. He sat immersed, and waited. This he had learned by the river, this one thing: to wait, to have patience, to listen. And he sat and listened, in the dust of the street, listened to his heart as it beat wearily and sadly, waited for a voice. For many hours he huddled listening, saw no more images, sunk into the emptiness, let himself sink, without seeing a path. And when he felt the wound burning, he silently spoke the Om, filled himself with Om. The monks in the garden saw him, and as he had huddled for many hours and the dust was collecting on his gray hair, one of them walked over and lay two pisang fruits down before him. The old man did not see him.

From this rigid state he was awoken by a hand that touched his shoulder. At once he recognized this touch, gentle, modest, and he came to. He rose and greeted Vasudeva, who had come after him. And as he looked into Vasudeva's friendly face, into the small wrinkles all filled with smiles, into the cheerful eyes, he smiled as well. He now saw the pisang fruits lying before him, picked them up, gave one to the ferryman, ate the other himself. Then he walked silently with Vasudeva back into the forest, returned home to the ferry. Neither spoke of what had happened today, neither spoke the name of the boy, neither spoke of his escape, neither spoke of the wound. In the hut, Siddhartha lay down on his bed and after a while, when Vasudeva came to him to offer him a bowl of coconut milk, he found him already sleeping.

OM

For a long time the wound still burned. Some travelers that Siddhartha had to ferry across the river had a son or a daughter with them and he saw none of them without envying them, without thinking: "So many, so many thousands possess this sweetest happiness—why don't I? Even wicked people, even thieves and robbers have children, and love them, and are loved by them, only I do not." So simple, so senseless had his thinking become, so similar had he become to the child-people.

He saw the people differently now than he did before, less cleverly, less proudly, and therefore all the more warmly, more curiously, more empathetically. When he ferried the ordinary sort of travelers—child-people, tradesmen, warriors, women-folk—these people did not seem as strange to him as they once had: he understood them, he understood and shared their life, governed not by thoughts and insights but solely by instincts and desires; he felt like they did. Although he was close to perfection and bearing his final wound, it still seemed to him that these child-people were his brothers; their vanities, desires, and absurdities lost their absurdity for him, became comprehensible, became endearing, became even worthy of respect for him. A mother's blind love for her child, a vain father's stupid, blind pride in his only little son, a young, vain woman's blind, wild pursuit of ornaments and of the admiring eyes of men, all these urges, all this childishness, all these simple, foolish, but enormously strong, strongly living, strongly prevailing instincts and desires were now no longer childishness for Siddhartha; he saw people living for their sake, saw them achieving endless feats for their sake, taking journeys, waging wars, suffering endlessly, enduring endlessly, and he could love them for it. He saw the life, the living, the indestructible, the Brahman in each of their passions, each of their deeds. Worthy of love and admiration were these people in their blind loyalty, their blind strength and tenacity. They were lacking nothing, the knowing and thinking man had nothing that they lacked aside from one single trifle, one single tiny little thing: consciousness, the conscious thought of the oneness of all life. And Siddhartha even doubted at times whether this knowledge, this thought, should be valued so highly, wondering whether perhaps it could be a childishness of the thinking people, of the thinking child-people. In all other things, the worldly people were the wise men's equals, were often far superior to them, just as animals in their tough, unwavering way of doing what is necessary can appear at times to be superior to people.

Slowly blossoming, slowly ripening within Siddhartha was the insight, the knowledge of what wisdom really was, what the goal of his long search was. It was nothing but a readiness of the soul, a skill, the secret art of being able to think the thought of oneness every moment, in the midst of living, to feel the oneness and breathe it in. Gradually this blossomed within him, shone back at him from Vasudeva's aged childlike face: harmony, knowledge of the eternal perfection of the world, smiling, oneness.

But the wound still burned; with longing and bitterness Siddhartha thought of his son, nurtured his love and tenderness in his heart, let the pain gnaw at him, committed all the follies of love. This flame would not extinguish on its own.

And one day, when the wound was burning intensely, Siddhartha crossed the river, driven by longing, got out of the boat with the intention of going to the city and looking for his son. The river was flowing gently and quietly, it was the dry season, but its voice sounded strange: it was laughing! It was distinctly laughing. The river was laughing, it was brightly and clearly laughing at the old ferryman. Siddhartha stopped, leaned over the water in order to hear better, and saw his face reflected in the calmly streaming water, and in this reflected face there was something that stirred his memory, something forgotten, and when he thought about it, he found it: this face resembled another one that he had once known and loved and also feared. It resembled the face of his father, the Brahmin. And he remembered how he, ages ago, when he was a youth, had forced his father to let him go to join the penitents, how he had taken leave of him, how he had left and never again returned. Had his father not also suffered the same pain that he was now suffering on account of his son? Had his father not long since died, alone, without ever having seen his son again? Must he not expect this same fate? Was this not a comedy, a strange and stupid thing, this repetition, this running in a fatal circle?

The river laughed. Yes, it was so, everything returned that had not been suffered and resolved to the end: the same pain was always being suffered over and over. Siddhartha, however, climbed back into the boat and rowed back to the hut, thinking of his father, thinking of his son, with the river laughing at him, in conflict with himself, inclined to despair, and no less inclined to join in and laugh aloud at himself and the entire world. Oh, the wound was still not blossoming, his heart was still resisting fate, cheerfulness and victory were still not shining from his pain. But he felt hope, and when he returned to the hut he felt an unconquerable desire to open himself to Vasudeva, to show everything to him, to tell everything to him, the master of listening.

Vasudeva sat in the hut weaving a basket. He no longer rowed the ferryboat, his eyes were beginning to grow weak, and not only his eyes but also his arms and hands. Unchanged and blossoming were only the joy and the serene benevolence of his face.

Siddhartha sat down beside the old man, slowly he began to speak. That which they had never spoken of, he now told him, of his journey to the city, back then, of the burning wound, of his envy at the sight of happy fathers, of his knowledge of the foolishness of such desires, of his futile struggle to resist them. He reported everything, he could say everything, even the most embarrassing things, everything could be said, everything could be shown, he could tell everything.

He showed his wound, spoke also of today's flight, how he crossed the water, childish refugee, intending to walk to the city, how the river had laughed.

As he spoke, spoke for a long time, as Vasudeva listened with a still face, Siddhartha felt Vasudeva's listening more strongly than ever before; he felt his pain, his fears flowing away, his secret hope flowing away and coming back toward him from the other side. To show his wound to this listener was the same as bathing it in the river until it became cool and one with the river. As he continued to speak, continued to confide and confess, Siddhartha felt more and more that it was no longer Vasudeva, no longer a person who was listening to him, that this motionless listener soaked in his confession as does a tree the rain, that this motionless one was the river itself, that he was god himself, that he was the Eternal itself. And as Siddhartha stopped thinking of himself and of his wound, this insight into Vasudeva's altered being took possession of him, and the more he felt it and entered into it, the less strange it became, the more he realized that everything was as it should be and natural, that Vasudeva had been this way for a long time, almost always, but that he himself had not quite realized it, and yes, that he himself was hardly different from him any longer. He felt that he now saw the old Vasudeva the way the people see the gods, and that this could not be lasting; he began in his heart to take leave of Vasudeva. As he did, he continued to speak on.

When he had finished speaking, Vasudeva focused his kind, somewhat weakened gaze upon him, did not speak, silently shone love and cheerfulness toward him, understanding and knowledge. He took Siddhartha's hand, led him to the seat on the riverbank, sat down with him, smiled at the river.

"You heard it laughing," he said. "But you did not hear everything. Let us listen, you will hear more."

They listened. Gently rang the many-voiced song of the river. Siddhartha looked into the water and in the streaming water images appeared to him: his father appeared, lonely, mourning for his son; he himself appeared, lonely, also bound by the bonds of longing for the distant son; his son appeared, he too lonely, the boy eagerly charging down the burning path of his young desires; each focused on their goal, each possessed by their goal, each suffering. The river sang with a voice of sorrow, it sang longingly, longingly it flowed toward its goal, its voice a lament.

"Do you hear?" asked Vasudeva's mute gaze. Siddhartha nodded.

"Listen better!" whispered Vasudeva.

Siddhartha made an effort to listen better. The image of his father, his own image, the image of his son flowed into one another; also Kamala's image appeared and dissolved, and the image of Govinda, and other images, and flowed into one another. All became the river, all striving as the river to reach their goal, longingly, eagerly, suffering, and the river's voice rang full of longing, full of burning woe, full of unquenchable desire. The river strove toward its goal, Siddhartha saw it rushing, the river, that was made of himself and his loved ones and of all the people he had ever seen, all the waves and waters were rushing, suffering, toward their goals, many goals, the waterfall, the lake, the rapid, the ocean, and all goals were reached, and each was followed by a new one, and the water became steam and rose to the sky, became rain and plunged down from the sky, became spring, became stream, became river, strove anew, flowed anew. But the longing voice had changed. It still resounded, sorrowfully, searchingly, but other voices joined it, voices of joy and sorrow, good and evil voices, laughing and mourning, a hundred voices, a thousand voices.

Siddhartha listened. He was now all listener, entirely immersed in listening, entirely empty, entirely absorbing, he felt that he had now learned to listen. He had heard all this often before, the many voices in the river, but today it sounded new. Already he could no longer distinguish the many voices, not the joyful from the weeping, not the child's from the man's, they all belonged together, the lament of longing and the laughter of the wise, the scream of anger and the moaning of the dying, everything was one, everything was interwoven and interlinked, entwined a thousand times. And all of this together, all voices, all goals, all longing, all suffering, all desire, all good and evil, all of it together was the world. All of it together was the river of occurrences, was the music of life. And when Siddhartha listened attentively to this river, this thousand-voiced song, when he listened neither for the sorrow nor for the laughter, when instead of binding his soul to one voice and entering into it with his Self, he heard all of them, heard the entirety, the oneness, then the great song of the thousand voices consisted of one single word, which was Om: perfection.

"Do you hear?" Vasudeva's gaze asked again.

Vasudeva's smile shone brightly, floated radiantly above all the wrinkles in his old face, as the Om floated above all the voices of the river. His smile shone brightly as he looked at his friend, and Siddhartha's face now shone brightly with the same smile. His wound blossomed, his sorrow shone, his Self had flowed into the Oneness.

In this hour Siddhartha stopped struggling with fate, stopped suffering. Upon his face blossomed the serenity of knowledge that is no longer opposed by any will, that knows perfection, that is in agreement with the river of occurrences, with the current of life, full of compassion, full of shared pleasure, given to the currents, belonging to the Oneness.

When Vasudeva rose from the seat on the riverbank, when he looked into Siddhartha's eyes and saw the serenity of knowledge shining in them, he touched his shoulder quietly with his hand, in his careful and tender way, and said: "I have waited for this hour, dear friend. Now that it has come, let me go. I have waited for this hour for a long time, I have been the ferryman Vasudeva for a long time. Now it is enough. Farewell hut, farewell river, farewell Siddhartha!"

Siddhartha bowed deeply before the one departing.

"I knew it," he said quietly. "You will go into the forest?"

"I am going into the forest, I am going into oneness," spoke Vasudeva, radiant.

Radiant, he walked away; Siddhartha watched him go. With deep joy, with deep solemnity he watched him go, saw his steps full of peace, saw his head full of brilliance, saw his figure full of light.

GOVINDA

Together with other monks, Govinda lingered during a resting period in the pleasure grove that the courtesan Kamala had given to Gautama's disciples. He heard talk of an old ferryman who lived beside the river, a day's journey from the grove, and who was considered by many to be a wise man. When Govinda continued on his way, he chose the path to the ferry, eager to see this ferryman. For although he had lived his entire life according to the rules, and was regarded with reverence by the younger monks on account of his age and modesty, the restlessness and the searching in his heart were still not extinguished.

He came to the river, he asked the old man to take him across, and when they climbed out of the boat on the other side, he said to the old man: "You have shown us monks and pilgrims much kindness, you have ferried many of us across. Are you, ferryman, not also a seeker searching for the right path?"

Said Siddhartha, smiling with his old eyes: "You call yourself a seeker, O Venerable One, and yet are so advanced in years and wear the robe of Gautama's monks?"

"Indeed, I am old," said Govinda, "but I have never stopped searching. I shall never stop searching, this appears to be my destiny. You, it appears to me, have also sought. Would you care to tell me a word, Honorable One?"

Said Siddhartha: "What could I have to tell you, Venerable One? Perhaps that you seek all too much? That all your seeking is keeping you from finding?"

"How can this be?" asked Govinda.

"When someone seeks," said Siddhartha, "then it happens easily that his eye only sees the thing that he is seeking, that he is not capable of finding anything or letting anything enter into him because he only thinks of that which he seeks, because he has a goal, because he is obsessed with the goal. Seeking means: having a goal. Finding, however, means: being free, being open, having no goal. You, Venerable One, may indeed be a seeker, striving to reach your goal; you do not see many things that are just before your eyes."

"I do not yet fully understand," asked Govinda. "How do you mean this?"

Said Siddhartha: "Once, O Venerable One, many years ago, you were at this river before and found by the river a sleeping man, and sat beside him to watch over his sleep. But you did not, O Govinda, recognize the sleeping man."

Amazed, like one enchanted, the monk looked into the ferryman's eyes.

"Are you Siddhartha?" he asked in a shy voice. "I would not have recognized you this time either! I greet you sincerely, Siddhartha, I am sincerely happy to see you again! You have changed a lot, my friend—and so now you have become a ferryman?"

Siddhartha laughed warmly. "A ferryman, yes. Some people must change themselves many times, Govinda, must wear all kinds of garments, and I am one such person, dear friend. I welcome you, Govinda, spend the night in my hut."

Govinda spent the night in the hut and slept upon the bed that had once been Vasudeva's bed. He had many questions for the friend of his youth; Siddhartha had to tell him many stories from his life.

The next morning, when it was time to begin the day's journey, Govinda said, not without hesitation, the words: "Before I continue on my way, Siddhartha, allow me one more question. Do you have a teaching? Do you have a belief or knowledge that you follow, that helps you to live and do what is right?"

Said Siddhartha: "You know, dear friend, that already as a young man, back when we lived among the penitents in the forest, I had already begun to distrust teachers and teachings and to turn my back on them. I have stayed with this. But I have still had many teachers since then. A beautiful courtesan was my teacher for a long time, and a rich merchant was my teacher, and several dice players. Once, a wandering disciple of Buddha was my teacher; he sat beside me when I had fallen asleep in the forest, on a pilgrimage. From him I also learned, to him I am also grateful, very grateful. But most of all, I learned here from this river, and from my predecessor, the ferryman Vasudeva. He was a very simple man, Vasudeva, he was not a thinker, but he knew what was necessary just as well as Gautama: he was a Perfect One, a saint."

Govinda said: "It seems to me, O Siddhartha, that you are still fond of a little mockery. I believe you and know that you did not follow a teacher. But have you yourself not found, if not a teaching, then certain thoughts, certain insights that belong to you and help you to live? If you would tell me something about them, you would bring joy to my heart."

Said Siddhartha: "I have had thoughts, yes, and insights, now and again. I have sometimes felt, for an hour or for a day, knowledge within myself just as one feels life within one's heart. There were many thoughts, but it would be difficult for me to share them with you. You see, my Govinda, this is one of the thoughts that I have found: Wisdom cannot be conveyed. Wisdom that a wise man attempts to convey always sounds like foolishness."

"Are you joking?" asked Govinda.

"I am not joking. I am saying what I have found. One can convey knowledge but not wisdom. One can find it, one can live it, one can be carried by it, one can do wonders with it, but one cannot speak it or teach it. This was what I sometimes suspected already as a youth, what drove me away from the teachers. I have found one thought, Govinda, that you will also take for a joke or foolishness, but which is my best thought. It is: for every truth, the opposite is equally true! It is namely so: a truth can only be spoken and shrouded in words when it is one-sided. Everything is one-sided that can be thought with thoughts and spoken with words, everything one-sided, everything half, everything lacking wholeness, roundness, oneness. When the sublime Gautama spoke of the world in his Teaching, he had to divide it into Sansara and Nirvana, into illusion and truth, into suffering and redemption. One can't avoid it, there is no other way for he who wishes to teach. The world itself, however, that which is Being all around and within us, is never one-sided. Never is a person or a deed entirely Sansara or entirely Nirvana, never is a person entirely holy or entirely sinful. It seems so because we are subject to the illusion that time is something real. Time is not real, Govinda; I have experienced this again and again. And if time is not real, the span that seems to lie between the world and eternity, between suffering and bliss, between evil and good, is also an illusion."

"How can this be?" asked Govinda fearfully.

"Listen well, dear friend, listen well! The sinner, that I am and that you are, he is a sinner, but he will one day be Brahman again, he will one day reach Nirvana, will be a Buddha—and now behold: this 'one day' is an illusion, is only an allegory! The sinner is not on the path to Buddhahood, he is not involved in a development, although our thinking does not know how to imagine things otherwise. No, in this sinner, the future Buddha already exists, now and today, all his future is already there; you must worship the future, the potential, the hidden Buddha in him, in you, in everyone. The world, friend Govinda, is not incomplete, or in the midst of a long path to completion. No, it is complete at every moment, all sins already carry grace within, all small children already have the aged within, all infants death, all dying men eternal life. It is not possible for any person to see how far someone else is on their path; in the thief and dice player waits Buddha, in the Brahmin waits the thief. There is, in deep meditation, the possibility of suspending time, to see all life that has been, is being, and will be simultaneously, and there everything is good, everything complete, everything is Brahman. This is why that which *is* seems good to me. Death seems like life, sin like holiness, cleverness like foolishness; everything must be this way, everything requires only my approval, only my willingness, my loving consent, for me it is good this way, it can never harm me. I have experienced with my body and my soul that I very much needed sin, I needed lust, the striving for possessions, vanity, and I needed the most shameful despair to learn to give up resisting, to learn to love the world, to no longer compare it to some world that I wished for, that I imagined, some kind of perfection that I had thought up, but to leave it as it is, and to love it and be happy to belong to it—these, O Govinda, are some of the thoughts that have come to my mind."

Siddhartha bent down, picked up a stone from the ground, and weighed it in his hand.

"This here," he said playing, "is a stone, and in a certain amount of time it will perhaps become earth, and from earth it will become a plant, or an animal or person. Earlier I would have said: this stone is only a stone, it is worthless, it belongs to the world of Maya; but because in the cycle of transformations it may also become person and spirit, this is why I also grant it significance. This is how I may have thought before. But today I think: this stone is stone, it is also animal, it is also god, it is also Buddha, I do not venerate and love it because it once was or could become this or that, but because it has long since been and always is everything—and precisely this, that it is stone, that it appears to me now and today as stone. This is precisely why I love it and see value and meaning in each of its veins and hollows, in the yellow, in the gray, in the hardness, in the sound that it makes when I knock on it, in the dryness or dampness of its surface. There are stones that feel like oil or like soap, and others like leaves, others like sand, and each is special and prays Om in its own way, each is Brahman. But at the same time and to the same extent, each is stone, is oily or soapy, and precisely this is what pleases me and seems to me to be wonderful and worthy of adoration. But let me speak no more of it. The words are not good for the secret meaning; everything always becomes a bit different when one says it aloud, a bit distorted, a bit foolish—yes, and this is also very good and pleases me greatly, this I also very much agree with: that one person's treasure and wisdom always sounds like foolishness to the others."

Silently Govinda listened.

"Why did you tell me that about the stone?" he asked hesitantly after a pause.

"It happened unintentionally. Or perhaps what was meant was that I love the stone, and the river, and all these things that we behold and from which we can learn. I can love a stone, Govinda, and also a tree or a piece of bark. These are things, and one can love things. But I cannot love words. This is why teachings are nothing for me, they have no hardness, no softness, no colors, no edges, no smell, no taste, they have nothing but words. Perhaps it is this that is keeping you from finding peace, perhaps it is the many words. For even redemption and virtue, even Sansara and Nirvana, are only words,

Govinda. There is no thing that Nirvana could be; there is only the word Nirvana."

Said Govinda: "Nirvana is not only a word, my friend. It is a thought."

Siddhartha carried on: "A thought, that may be so. I have to admit, dear friend: I do not differentiate much between thoughts and words. To be honest, I also don't think very highly of thoughts. I think more highly of things. Here on this ferry-boat, for example, a man was my predecessor and teacher, a holy man, who believed for many years only in the river, nothing else. He had noticed that the river's voice spoke to him, he learned from it, it trained and taught him, the river seemed to him a god, and for many years he did not know that every wind, every cloud, every bird, every beetle is just as divine and knows and can teach just as much as the venerated river. But when this holy man went into the forest, he knew everything, knew more than you and I, without a teacher, without books, only because he had believed in the river."

Govinda said: "But is that which you call 'things' something real, something of substance? Is it not merely an illusion of Maya, merely image and semblance? Your stone, your tree, your river—are they realities?"

"This also," said Siddhartha, "does not trouble me much. Let the things be semblance or not; then I too am only semblance, and so they will always be my equals. That is what makes them so dear to me and venerable: they are my equals. This is why I can love them. And here is a teaching that you will laugh at: love, O Govinda, appears to me to be the main thing above all else. To figure out the world, to explain it, to condemn it, may be the task of great thinkers. For me, however, the only important thing is being able to love the world, not to condemn it, not to hate it and myself, but to be able to view it and myself and all beings with love and admiration and awe."

"This I understand," said Govinda. "But this is just what he, the Sublime One, recognized as illusion. He commands benevolence, lenience, compassion, tolerance, but not love; he forbade us to shackle our heart with love for earthly things."

"I know it," said Siddhartha; his smile shone golden. "I know it, Govinda. And behold, we are now in the midst of a thicket of opinions, in a dispute over words. For I cannot deny that my words about love stand in conflict, in apparent conflict, with Gautama's words. This is precisely why I distrust words so much, for I know that this conflict is an illusion. I know that I am in agreement with Gautama. How could He not also know love, He, who recognized all humanity in its transience, its insignificance, and still loved people so much that he devoted a long, laborious life solely to helping them, to teaching them! Even with him, even with your great teacher, I find the thing preferable to the words, his deeds and life more important than his speaking, the gesture of his hand more important than his opinions. I see his greatness not in speaking or in thinking, only in deeds, in life."

For a long time the two old men were silent. Then Govinda said as he bowed to take his leave: "I thank you, Siddhartha, that you have told me some of your thoughts. They are strange thoughts in part, not all of them were comprehensible to me right away. Be that as it may, I thank you and I wish you peaceful days."

Secretly, however, he thought to himself: this Siddhartha is a curious person, curious are the thoughts he utters, his teaching sounds foolish. The Sublime One's pure Teaching sounds different, clearer, purer, easier to understand, nothing that is strange, foolish, or ridiculous is included in it. But Siddhartha's hands and feet, his eyes, his brow, his breathing, his smile, his greeting, his gait, seem to me to be different from his thoughts. Never again, after our sublime Gautama entered into Nirvana, never again have I encountered a person about whom I felt: this is a saint. About him alone, this Siddhartha, have I felt this way. His teaching may be strange, his words may sound foolish, but his gaze and his hand, his skin and his hair, everything about him radiates a purity, radiates a calm, radiates a serenity and mildness and holiness that I have seen in no other person since the final death of our sublime teacher.

As Govinda thought these thoughts, with a conflict in his heart, he bent down once again to Siddhartha, drawn by love. He bowed deeply before the one sitting calmly.

"Siddhartha," he said, "we have become old men. It is unlikely that one of us will see the other again in this shape. I see, beloved friend, that you have found peace. I confess that I have not found it. Tell me, my honored friend, one more word, give me something that I can grasp, that I can understand! Give me something to take along on my path. It is often burdensome, my path; it is often dark, Siddhartha."

Siddhartha remained silent and continued to look at him with the same still smile. Govinda gazed rigidly into his face, with fear, with longing, with suffering, and eternal searching written in his gaze, eternal not-finding.

Siddhartha saw it and smiled.

"Lean toward me!" he whispered quietly into Govinda's ear. "Lean toward me here! Yes, even closer! Very close! Kiss me on the forehead, Govinda!"

As Govinda, astonished but still drawn by great love and premonition, obeyed his words, leaned toward him and touched his forehead with his lips, something wonderful happened to him. As his thoughts still lingered over Siddhartha's strange words, as he still attempted in vain and with reluctance to think away time, to imagine Nirvana and Sansara as one, as a certain contempt for his friend's words even fought within him with an immense love and reverence, this happened to him:

He no longer saw his friend Siddhartha's face, he saw instead other faces, many faces, a long succession, a streaming river of faces, of hundreds, of thousands, all coming and going, and yet all seemed to be there at once, all of them changing and renewing themselves constantly, and all of them were Siddhartha. He saw the face of a fish, of a carp, with its mouth opened in endless pain, a dying fish with breaking eyes—he saw the face of a newborn child, red and full of wrinkles, twisted to cry—he saw the face of a murderer, saw him stab a knife into a person's body—he saw, in the same second, this criminal kneeling in chains and his head being chopped off with one stroke of the executioner's sword—he saw the bodies of men and women naked in positions and struggles of raging love—he saw corpses laid out, still, cold, empty—he saw the heads of animals, of wild boars, of crocodiles, of elephants, of bulls, of birds—he saw gods, saw Krishna, saw Agni—he saw all these shapes and faces in a thousand connections to one another, each helping the other, loving them, hating them, destroying them, giving birth to them anew. Each was a wish to die, a passionately painful confession of transience, and yet none died, each one only transformed itself, was always born anew, always received a new face but without time having passed between one face and the other—and all these shapes and faces rested, flowed, generated themselves, swam away, and streamed together, and above all of them, constantly, was something thin, unsubstantial, but still existing, stretched like thin glass or ice, like a transparent skin, a shell or form or mask of water, and this mask smiled, and this mask was Siddhartha's smiling face, which he, Govinda, at just this same moment, was touching with his lips. And Govinda saw that this smile of the mask, this smile of oneness over all the streaming shapes, this smile of simultaneity over the thousand births and deaths, this smile of Siddhartha's was exactly identical, was exactly the same, still, fine, impenetrable, perhaps kind, perhaps mocking, wise, thousandfold smile of Gautama, the Buddha, as he himself had seen it a hundred times with awe. This, Govinda knew, is how Perfect Ones smile.

No longer knowing whether time existed, whether this display had lasted a second or a hundred years, no longer knowing whether a Siddhartha, whether a Gautama, whether I and you existed, injured in his innermost core as though by a divine arrow, whose injury tastes sweet, enchanted, and dispersed in his innermost core, Govinda stood a little while longer, leaned over Siddhartha's still face, which he had just kissed, which had just been the scene of all shapes, all Becoming, all Being. This face was unchanged after the depth of the thousandfold forms had closed again beneath its surface; he smiled silently, smiled quietly and gently, perhaps very kindly, perhaps very mockingly, just as *he* had smiled—the Sublime One.

Govinda bowed deeply. Tears of which he knew nothing streamed down his old face, like a fire; the feeling of the most intense love, the most humble reverence, burned in his heart. Deeply he bowed, down to the earth, before the one who sat motionless, whose smile reminded him of everything in his life that he had ever loved, everything in his life that had ever been dear and holy to him.

ACKNOWLEDGMENTS

The translator would like to express her gratitude to Jürgen and Marylou Pelzer, for their support; to Jan Weinert, for his insight and enthusiasm; and Utz and Luis Tayert, for their patience and inspiration.